Praise for

ANNETTE
BROADRICK

"Whether she's writing romantic suspense
or pure romance, Annette Broadrick always
tells a great story! I love her
tough but tender heroes!"
—Bestselling author Ann Major

"I love Annette Broadrick's books! They
make me laugh and cry and then laugh
again as she takes me on a whirlwind ride
toward a wonderfully happy ending."
—Award-winning author Paula Detmer Riggs

ANNETTE BROADRICK

believes in romance and the magic of life. Since 1984, Annette has shared her view of life and love with readers. In addition to being nominated by *Romantic Times* magazine as one of the Best New Authors of that year, she has also won the *Romantic Times* Reviewers' Choice Award for Best in its Series, the *Romantic Times* WISH award, and the *Romantic Times* magazine Lifetime Achievement Awards for Series Romance and Series Romantic Fantasy.

ANNETTE BROADRICK

Daddy's Angel

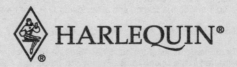 HARLEQUIN®

TORONTO • NEW YORK • LONDON
AMSTERDAM • PARIS • SYDNEY • HAMBURG
STOCKHOLM • ATHENS • TOKYO • MILAN • MADRID
PRAGUE • WARSAW • BUDAPEST • AUCKLAND

This book is dedicated to all those very special angels who devote their valuable time to the loving, nurturing and caring of a husband and/or children 365 days a year.

You know who you are. So does God.

ISBN 0-373-81077-6

DADDY'S ANGEL

Copyright © 1993 by Annette Broadrick.

This edition published by arrangement with Harlequin Books S.A.

® and TM are trademarks of the publisher. Trademarks indicated with ® are registered in the United States Patent and Trademark Office, the Canadian Trade Marks Office and in other countries.

www.eHarlequin.com

Printed in U.S.A.

Prologue

Noelle waited patiently.

Noelle St. Nichols had all the patience in the world. Of course, technically speaking, she wasn't part of the world.

Not exactly.

For several seasons now, she'd been a Christmas angel, the kind who presides at the very top of the Christmas tree each season.

Before accepting her present occupation, she'd enjoyed a multitude of varied assignments...all part of the training for novice angels. Not that people on earth understand the

extensive training each and every angel willingly pursues. Many people have absolutely
no conception that angels exist.

Of course most people have heard about
them, particularly at Christmastime. Whenever
the Christmas story is told, the listener hears
about the time when the angels appeared to
the shepherds, announcing the birth of the
baby Jesus.

Because of the special sense of love and
understanding that seems to fill the air around
Christmastime, some people—if asked—might
admit that quite possibly there really was a
time when there were angels who actually
talked to shepherds. If pressed, they might admit to believing that even in this day and age
there are angels who protect small children.

Few people, however, want to admit that
they could have a guardian angel, although
they might joke about the possibility.

Noelle had never been able to understand
how people could speak about guardian angels
as though they were a joke. How could
such an honorable profession be considered
amusing?

At one point in her training, her highest aspiration had been to become a guardian angel. She had diligently studied for her proposed calling and had been given several assignments that had resulted in less than spectacular results. She'd discovered that attempting to guide and protect a person who was determined to ignore that quiet voice within could be difficult—not to mention downright frustrating!

Noelle sighed and thought back over her long and varied career, which had been filled with unexpected twists and turns.

One of her less admirable traits was her impulsiveness.

She wouldn't be where she was today if she hadn't impulsively offered to fill in for a friend on this particular assignment.

How could she have known at the time the far-reaching effects her present occupation would have on her own goals and aspirations? Even if she could have foreseen the consequences, she wasn't certain she could have resisted the opportunity to be with children.

Children were her very special love. What

better way for her to be around them than to become part of their annual celebration of Christmas?

Small children still had memories of the time when they lived with the angels. They recognized her immediately. Consequently she had no difficulty communicating with them.

She'd been filled with excitement by the thought that she might be placed in a child's home and be given the opportunity to offer one or more children a refresher course on love and all its many aspects—such as compassion ... and caring ... understanding ... and sharing ... empathy ... and acceptance.

As far as she was concerned, one of her most sacred duties was to remind children of the larger significance of Christmas, that it was a magical time when love could produce miracles.

Children came into the world filled with a wondrous knowledge of all things. Unfortunately many of them forgot about the wonder and the magic of Christmas as they grew older, which was why Noelle St. Nichols chose to come to earth as a reminder. So she became a Christmas tree angel.

And fell head over heels in love.

She sighed, thinking of the series of events that had taken place for her since she had become a Christmas tree angel. So much had happened, both joyous and sad.

Bret Bishop had had an extraordinary effect on her. He had stolen her heart as surely as a train robber successfully empties a safe.

She winced at her unfortunate choice of metaphor. The train robber had been one of her earlier assignments as a guardian angel. He hadn't been one of her successes.

Her record carried as many failures as it did triumphs, although her supervisor continued to remind her that there was no such thing as a failure in their dimension...only lessons to be learned.

Falling in love certainly hadn't been part of her particular curriculum, but it had happened, even though Bret Bishop was unaware of her existence.

While she waited for her annual liberation from the attic, Noelle reminisced, reliving that time in her history when she had believed she would be filling in as a Christmas tree angel for only a few weeks.

She wore a shimmery white gown with a long full skirt that stood stiffly in a full circle around her. Her white-blond hair fell in waves to her waist and framed her face. A twinkling halo of brilliants encircled her head and in her left hand she carried a tiny, star-tipped wand.

For several days she'd entertained herself by sending waves of loving energy to the children who walked through the aisles of the department store where she was displayed. Rarely did she notice the adults until the day she heard someone say, "Bret, would you look at this?"

A young woman with short black curls framing her face paused in front of the tree ornament section where Noelle was prominently displayed. The man beside her obligingly glanced at Noelle.

Noelle looked back…and was a goner.

The first thing she noticed about Bret Bishop was his happiness. He glowed with it, especially whenever he looked at the woman beside him.

He was young, Noelle noted. A very fine specimen of manhood—his body perfectly proportioned, his face filled with integrity.

Noelle was certain she knew him...or had known him from some other dimension in space and time. Her reaction was much too strong not to have been forged in an earlier reality.

"She's something, isn't she, Patti?" he responded. His deep voice caused shivers along Noelle's spine.

"Wouldn't she be beautiful on top of our tree?"

Bret smiled, his teasing filled with love. "Honey, I don't know quite how to tell you this," he drawled, "but that angel, small as she is, would dwarf our puny li'l ol' tree."

"Then let's get a bigger tree," Patti promptly suggested.

"You're the one who said a miniature fir tree was all the two of us needed this year."

Patti looked up at him with an impish grin. "I know. I was thinking about this being our first Christmas." She touched his arm, her gaze imploring. "Darling, someday we'll have a family. Can't you just picture that little angel sitting on top of a tree, with all our children gathered around?"

He slipped his arm around her waist and tugged her closer to his side, placing a light kiss on her nose.

"*A-a-l-ll* our children?" he repeated, chuckling. "Sounds like you're planning to have dozens."

She tucked her fingers into the side belt loops of his snug-fitting jeans and peered up at him through her thick lashes. "I have a hunch that we have so much love to share we're going to want a houseful of babies, honey."

Bret's response to her throaty, deliberately provocative comment was laughter—rich, exuberant and filled with joy.

How could Noelle have resisted falling in love?

All right, so this couple didn't have children. So what? They were young, probably newlyweds and they understood what love and life and Christmas were truly about. Noelle hoped they would buy her, regardless of the size of their present tree. She wanted to be a part of their lives, to oversee a family that would grow and become an integral part of her present existence.

She also hoped to find a niche in the life of Bret Bishop. She would be content to see him each year, content to be a tiny part of his world.

Noelle got her wish. Bret and Patti took her home that very day, to a two-room apartment near the campus where he was attending his last year of college.

During that first Christmas season with Bret and Patti, Noelle learned of their hopes and dreams as they sat in front of the lighted tree each night and discussed plans for their future.

She discovered that Bret had been born on a ranch in central Texas. Patti had grown up nearby. They had been friends all their lives. Neither one had ever considered living anywhere other than in the familiar hills of central Texas.

When Bret's grandfather died when Bret was eighteen, he left his ranching property to his grandson. However, Bret's father had insisted that Bret get his education—learn the latest about agriculture and livestock breeding—before taking over the actual running of the place. Bret had married Patti the summer before his senior year knowing that as soon as he graduated, they would move to the ranch and live there full-time.

Patti had finished a two-year course of her own and had found a job in the college town until her husband finished with his schooling. Their apartment was like a dollhouse. Life for them their first year seemed almost like playing and not at all like being married. The small apartment often rang with their laughter.

Noelle blessed their first Christmas together and patiently waited throughout the next year, and all the years that followed, to spend those few very special weeks with her newly expanding family.

First came Chris, a stocky little boy with his mother's gray eyes and his father's flashing smile.

Two years later Brenda appeared, full of bounce and seemingly unlimited energy. She had her father's light brown hair and golden eyes.

Eventually Sally arrived—tiny, but with a strong will and healthy lungs.

Noelle introduced herself to each one of the

children and explained to them who she was and why she was a part of their household. As the years passed, each child came to her to share secret wishes and cherished dreams. She watched as each one grew older until first Chris, then eventually Brenda and Sally forgot how to speak with her…and how to listen for her voice.

Noelle would never forget the year when Bret and Patti were decorating the newest Christmas tree and Patti told Bret that, once again, she was pregnant.…

Bret stared at Patti in dismay. "Pregnant? But you can't be! Didn't the doctor say—"

Patti went up on tiptoe, wrapping her arms around his neck. "What do you mean, I can't be?" she whispered with a smile. "Is your memory already slipping, cowboy? Do I have to go into detail exactly when and how this happened?" She kissed him in her very special way.

She managed to distract him, as usual, but only for a few moments. When he pulled away from her, he was frowning. "How can you joke about it, honey? How could you forget about the rough time you had when you carried Sally? The doctor told us then that—"

She covered his mouth with her hand. "I know what the doctor said, Bret. But lots of things have changed. Sally is almost five, so my body's had plenty of time to rest and recuperate. Besides, there's been all kinds of medical advances since my last pregnancy. I'm not worried and I don't want you to be, either." She danced away from him, threw her arms wide and turned in a circle. "I'm so excited. Just think! We're going to have another Bishop to love. Sally will start preschool in the spring. By fall she'll be ready for the first grade. The house will be so empty."

She paused and looked around the room with all its boxes of decorations. "Just think, Bret. This time next year we'll have a baby in our home once again, one who'll be dazzled by all the lights and color." She returned to Bret's side and brushed her fingers against his cheek. "Please be happy, honey. I know it's a bit of a shock, but I didn't want to say anything to you until I found out for sure. I wanted my news to be a special Christmas surprise for everybody.'' Her voice dropped to a whisper and tears filled her eyes. ''I can't think of anything I want more than to have another one of your children to love.''

He took her hand and gently placed a kiss in her palm. ''Honey, if this is what you want, then I'm happy, too.'' He gathered her in his arms as though she were made of the most fragile porcelain. ''All I've ever wanted was for you to be happy.''

''How could I not be happy? I have everything I could possibly want in my life—you and the children. I feel truly blessed.''

He shook his head, humbled by her courage and her determination. ''I love you, Patti Bishop,'' he murmured, holding her close.

''I love you, too, Bret. More than I can possibly say.''

Unfortunately their love for each other wasn't enough to keep Patti alive.

She was careful.

She followed the doctor's instructions.

She did everything she was supposed to do.

But her heart gave out without warning during the delivery of her second son. The skilled medical staff was unable to resuscitate her.

Noelle knew the events of that year despite the fact that she was packed carefully away with all the other decorations.

She felt Bret's pain at the loss of his beloved wife.

She felt his bewilderment when faced with the prospect of trying to raise four children on his own.

She felt his anger that God could have allowed such a thing to happen.

The newborn was a healthy little boy with his mother's black curls and gray eyes. Bret gave him the name Patti had picked for a boy—Travis.

Travis was four months old his first Christmas. If the older children hadn't insisted, Bret wouldn't have put up a tree that year. He found the season too painful a reminder of other years when Patti had been by his side.

The children missed their mother with a heartbroken intensity. Having the new baby to care for kept them going. Travis became their focal point. Taking care of him helped to heal their pain and ease their loss.

Three more years had passed and it was Christmastime once again, the fourth Christmas the Bishop family had spent without Patti. Noelle wanted to weep at the harsh changes that had taken place in Bret.

The laughing young man she'd first caught sight of all those years ago was gone, never to be seen again. In his place was a grim-faced rancher with overwhelming duties and responsibilities.

Bret had adjusted to his new way of life in some ways. He'd grown accustomed to being on his own with the children. He made certain he was there whenever they needed him. He planned his work schedule around their school schedules. He watched over them and supervised them.

What saddened Noelle the most was that over the years Bret had lost more than his mate....

Bret had lost his belief in the goodness of life.

Bret had abandoned all his hopes and dreams.

Noelle knew that yet another upheaval was soon to cause additional problems for the Bishop family. Unfortunately, as a mere Christmas tree angel she didn't have the jurisdiction to change certain events that had already been set into motion. She understood that every seemingly random event had a positive reason and result behind it. However, she knew that Bret wouldn't see the event in that light. He would see another burden placed on his shoulders.

She was afraid for him…afraid he would falter under his grim load of responsibilities because he'd lost sight of the very things that could lighten the burdens for him.

Somehow, someway, she wanted to be able to help him—to ease his load, to help him regain some of his beliefs about life, to help him to understand how things have a way of working out if we only give them a chance.

If we only believe.

Noelle contacted her supervisor to discuss the present situation in the Bishop household. She had a request to make—a very special request—one that was most unusual but because of the upcoming emergency, most necessary.

She knew the risks. As an angel she had never taken human form, never experienced human emotions, never been plagued by earthly considerations. She knew there would be limitations placed on her. She knew that, if she was given permission to take a more active role in the Bishop family, she would have to return to her original form no later than midnight on Christmas Eve.

She didn't know if that would give her enough time to help Bret. She only knew that she had to make the effort before he gave up on life completely.

She had to try.

Chapter One

Dark clouds rolled along the northern horizon, adding an urgency to Bret's movements. He gave the barbed wire an extra twist of his wrist, then wearily straightened and looked along the fence he'd recently mended.

No doubt a deer had pulled the top strand loose while bounding across the fence, causing the line to sag. He'd been checking all the fence lines of his ranch for the past several days. Some of the terrain was too rugged for him to use his pickup truck, his usual mode of conveyance. For the last two days he'd ridden Hercules.

Perhaps traveling around the ranch on horseback had prompted the recurrence of his memories of Patti. After all, Patti had given Hercules to him. She'd always enjoyed riding with him whenever she could get away for a few hours.

No doubt his saddling up Hercules and riding him yesterday had triggered the dreams he'd had last night.

He'd dreamed that Patti was alive. She'd been there next to him, holding him, talking to him, loving him.

His dream had seemed so real.

In it he told her that he thought she'd died. They laughed about such a silly idea. She'd held him in her arms and told him that she would never leave him. Not ever.

In the first seconds of awakening that morning he'd reached for her with joy in his heart, glad to be through with the nightmare of doing without her, only to find the other side of the bed empty.

He'd opened his eyes and realized the truth.

Patti was gone. She'd been gone for more than three years now.

No doubt his vivid dream the night before had caused the ache of missing her to be so strong today. He'd been feeling her loss all day in the same way he'd felt during those first black months when he hadn't believed he could go on without her.

A soft whine and the familiar weight leaning against his knee called Bret back to the present. He glanced down and rubbed his hand over Rex's head, glad for the German shepherd's company.

Even though the dog was getting up in years, he continued to follow Bret around the ranch, generally riding in the truck cab when it was raining or cold.

"Yeah, I know, old man," he murmured. "The wind's picking up and we've got a ways to go before we're home, with no truck heater to take the chill off."

Bret glanced around, seeing the gusts of wind create eddies of silt around them. He readjusted his broad-brimmed hat, pulling it low over his eyes, and headed over to where the horse waited.

The creak of the leather made a familiar

sound as he mounted the horse and gathered the reins in his gloved hand. He glanced to the north, narrowing his eyes as he measured the swiftness of the clouds racing toward him.

Those clouds looked ominous, threatening cold wind and icy rain. He didn't want to get caught in the hills when the rain hit. The footing among the rocks and cacti was dangerous enough in the best of conditions. Hopefully they would make it to the ranch road before the threatened downpour reached them.

Bret started down through the heavy underbrush of the rock-strewn hillside. Rex followed close behind.

Now that he was headed home, Bret's thoughts raced on ahead to his family, his expression growing more grim.

Chris had reminded him over breakfast this morning that they needed to get a tree before the yearly shipment of firs were all picked over. Chris, especially, insisted on keeping all the family traditions Patti had started. Even to the point of dragging out the same decorations year after year.

Thinking about the decorations reminded

Bret of the year he'd suggested to Patti that they should replace the bedraggled-looking Christmas tree angel they'd found the first Christmas they were married.

The tiny figure had lost the tip of one of her wings, her dress hung limp and the glitter had long since disappeared from her halo. Patti had been shocked and incensed that he would suggest such a thing. The angel was part of the Bishop Christmas tradition.

Now the children were just as bad about adhering to tradition. Christmas season didn't officially begin in the Bishop household until the tree was up, decorated and Bret had placed the angel with great ceremony at the top.

If Chris had his way, Bret would be up on the stepladder tonight, clutching the tiny ornament in his hand.

Bret had tried to explain that he didn't have time to go to town today, that he had too many other things to do. That's when Chris had asked if he could get Roy to take him to get the tree.

Bret didn't know what he would have done during the past three years without Roy Baker.

The ranch hand originally had been a part of the crew that worked for Bret's father ever since Bret had been a teenager. When Patti died, Roy—with no commotion—had moved to Bret's ranch and taken over the daily chores around the place. He knew as much about ranching as anybody in the district, but had never wanted the responsibility of his own place.

Roy was exactly the kind of friend Bret had needed during that black time after Patti's death, when Bret hadn't been certain he could survive without Patti by his side.

Roy had filled in wherever he was needed. A shy man only a few years older than Bret, Roy understood what needed to be done to keep the ranch in working order without Bret having to mention it.

Bret had been grateful for the help. They had never discussed whether the move would be temporary or permanent, but during the past three years Roy had settled into the small house that was part of the ranch buildings and become an integral part of the Bishop family circle.

Bringing a brand-new motherless child home from the hospital had been a painful and traumatic time for all of them. Bret hated to think what they would have done if fate, in the form of another lifelong friend, hadn't come to his rescue.

Freda Wilkenson had spent her early youth caring for her invalid mother and had never had time to develop a social life of her own. A few years older than Bret, Freda, timid and soft-spoken, approached him with a suggestion a few days after he'd brought Travis home.

Her mother had recently passed away and Freda felt lost with nothing to do to fill her empty days. She offered to move out to the ranch as housekeeper and to look after the children.

Accepting her offer of help had saved his sanity.

Bret knew that he couldn't have gotten through these past three years without the help of Roy and Freda. They had been there for him, encouraging him to establish some kind of life for his children during those days when all he'd wanted to do was to saddle up and keep on riding until he fell off the edge of the world.

Eventually he'd learned a very important lesson—a person couldn't feel sorry for himself for long when he had four children who needed his attention and care.

He still saw Patti in the silvery-gray flash of Chris's eyes...and caught a glimpse of her sparkling mischievousness in Brenda and Sally. But it was Travis who repeatedly pulled at his heartstrings. As though to make up for her loss, Patti had somehow passed on to her youngest son not only her black curls and features, but her gentle and loving personality as well.

Travis didn't talk much. With three older siblings, he didn't have to, since all of them had a habit of anticipating his every want and need. Despite the attention, he wasn't spoiled. He was just a happy little boy who offered his unconditional love to everyone around him.

Travis had listened to the girls over breakfast that morning as they asked when they were going to go shopping. He had stopped them all by asking if he was going to get to see Santa at the mall again this year. No one had thought Travis could have remembered his visit last Christmas, but obviously he had.

In an effort to gain some time, Bret had agreed to let Chris ask Roy to take him to town today to buy a tree, but only if Roy didn't have something else he needed to do.

Bret knew he was being a coward. He knew he should have agreed to take Chris into town, himself. It was just that Christmas never seemed to get any easier for him. He wished he could disappear until all the fuss of the season was behind him for another year.

He hated having to go into town for supplies between Thanksgiving and New Year's. Shiny tinsel streamers and giant red bells arched across the main streets of the small ranching community where they did most of their shopping. Every store he entered had its own display, generally accompanied by Christmas music.

There was just no getting away from the music. Even the country music station he listened to in the truck interspersed the current hits being played with familiar voices singing traditional songs.

A person couldn't get away from the reminders, no matter how much he tried.

A strong gust of wind grabbing at his hat brought Bret jarringly back to the present. He reached up and once more tugged the brim down low over his eyes.

Looking around, he noticed that while he'd been lost in thought, they'd managed to reach the dirt road that led back to the ranch buildings. Bret signaled the horse by subtly shifting his weight. Hercules immediately responded with ground-eating strides and Rex loped along beside them.

They reached the ranch buildings minutes before the storm hit. Safely inside the barn, Bret watched from the wide doorway as large hail bounced off the ground and the surrounding buildings. He breathed a thankful prayer that he'd gotten home when he did.

He took his time unsaddling Hercules and cooling him down before he wiped the horse dry and fed him. Although he could always explain to Freda and the kids that he'd been waiting for the first of the front to pass by, he knew the truth.

He dreaded going inside. If Roy hadn't taken Chris to town when he got home from school, then Bret knew he'd have to do so as soon as they ate.

If Roy had taken Chris to town, then Bret would have to help decorate the tree tonight. He knew he was putting off the inevitable. Sooner or later he would have to go into the house and face whatever festivities the family had planned for the evening.

By the time Bret sprinted across the wide expanse between the barn and house the hail had been replaced by pounding, icy rain splashing mud and turning the ground into a slippery quagmire.

He took the back-porch steps two at a time, then paused beneath the shelter of the roof to wipe off the bottoms of his boots before entering Freda's spotless kitchen. He removed his gloves and opened the door, already anticipating a cup of Freda's coffee to help remove the chill.

The first thing he noticed when he opened the door was the dark kitchen. The kitchen was the heart of their home, and its light generally came on first thing in the morning and stayed on until the last thing at night.

Today it was dark and deserted.

Bret absently brushed his hat off his head and hung it and his coat on a set of hooks beside the back door, next to the children's jackets. He noted that Chris's coat wasn't there, which probably meant that Chris and Roy hadn't returned from town, but didn't explain why Freda wasn't in the kitchen preparing supper.

"Hello?" he called. "Anybody home?"

Bret heard scrambling upstairs and the clattering of feet on the wooden stairs. At least somebody was here.

Eleven-year-old Brenda was the first to appear. Her golden eyes were wide with concern. Bret had a sudden sense of unease flash over him, which was confirmed with her first words.

"Dad! Thank goodness you're home! You'll never guess what happened this afternoon!"

Since his daughter was known for speaking in exclamations whenever she was excited,

Bret tried not to let her delivery cause him to jump to premature conclusions before hearing some details. Obviously something had happened out of their normal routine.

Eight-year-old Sally arrived immediately behind her sister, looking worried. However, Bret felt a strong sense of unease when three-year-old Travis came in clutching his familiar stuffed giraffe by its long neck, his eyes red from crying and his face pale. Bret knelt down on one knee and Travis ran into his arms, burying his face in Bret's neck.

Bret fought a surge of panic. The three younger children were obviously all right. It had to be...

"What happened? Is Chris—"

Brenda rushed into speech. "Chris and Roy had to take Freda to the hospital a while ago. She fell and Roy's afraid maybe she broke her leg or her hip or something. Oh, Dad! It was awful! She was in the kitchen and Roy thinks she must have stepped on some tree needles or something that dropped on the floor when they brought the tree inside and she didn't see it. Roy checked her as best as he could, then he called the doctor and the doctor said for him to get her to the hospital.'' She finally had to pause for a breath.

Bret stood, still holding Travis in his arms. In a quiet voice, which effectively disguised his growing sense of panic, he asked, "How long ago did this happen?''

Sally was the one who answered. "Almost two hours ago. We promised Freda we'd keep Travis entertained until you got back home and we did, but now he's saying he's hungry and we weren't sure what we should do.''

Brenda responded. "Of course we knew what to do, Dad. It isn't like I don't know how to cook or anything. But you told us not to have any fire going when an adult wasn't here, so I've been waiting, thinking you'd be home soon.''

Bret stroked her head with his hand. "Thanks, honey. I'm glad you remembered.''

"We could have sandwiches, couldn't we?'' Sally asked, glaring at her sister.

"That's a good idea,'' Bret said. "Why don't you make some while I call the hospital and see what I can find out about Freda?'' He gave Travis a quick hug, then set him in his high chair. With quick strides Bret headed down the hallway to his office, where he could talk in private.

The closest hospital was almost fifty miles away. Although the facility was small, several doctors drove from the surrounding large cities—Austin and San Antonio—to provide additional services to the sparsely populated hill country. He knew that Freda would receive excellent care there. What he was concerned about at the moment was the seriousness of her injuries.

As soon as he got through to the hospital Bret had Roy paged. He drummed his fingers on the desk, waiting what seemed like hours before Roy finally came on the line.

"How is she?"

Roy laughed, which eased Bret's tension considerably. "That woman's too feisty for her own good, boss. She's insisting she's got to get back home tonight, that she's got too much to do and that the children shouldn't be left alone. You know what she's like."

"Can you tell me what happened? The girls

were a little excited and I'm not sure I understood.''

"She stepped on something slippery and her foot went out from under her. Me and Chris had been trailing back and forth through there, bringing in the tree and all, and it's my guess we tracked something inside the house and she didn't see it in time to avoid it. It wouldn't have been so bad but she fell wrong—all awkwardlike. From the pain she was in I pretty much figured she'd broke a bone.''

"Is that what the doctors say?''

"Yep, her leg's definitely broken. They're ordering further tests, including more X rays, to look for anything else that might have been injured. I called Freda's sister in Austin to let her know about it, so she's on her way over here to sit with her.''

"Did the doctor say how long she would need to stay in the hospital?''

"He wants to keep her for several days, which has got Freda all upset, let me tell you.''

"You tell Freda that I want her to stop worrying about me and the kids. We'll do just fine. I want her to rest and recuperate. Tell her to

lie back and enjoy being waited on for a
change…to pretend she's on vacation.''

"Some vacation,'' Roy muttered.

"I know. I take it that Chris is still there
with you?''

"You bet he is. I don't know what I would
have done without that boy this afternoon. He
was right there helping me with Freda as calm
as you please just like he was a growed up
man and knew exactly what to do. I was
downright impressed by the way he kept his
head and all. That son of yours is growing up
real fast.''

"I know.''

"I never realized it until we was helpin' to
get Freda in my truck, but that dang kid is
almost as tall as I am,'' Roy said, his amazement plain. "When did that happen?''

"I noticed the same thing a day or so ago,
Roy. I guess that's what happens when you
keep feedin' 'em.''

"I keep threat'ning to put a brick on his
head, but it don't seem to do much good.''

Bret looked at his watch. "How much
longer do you intend to stay at the hospital?''

"Until the doctor tells me what these last X-rays show. Then I'll take the kid out and buy him something to eat before we head home."

Bret massaged his forehead, absently noting a headache he hadn't been aware of until now. "Sounds like a good plan to me."

"At least we managed to get that tree set in its stand before Freda fell. Maybe you and the girls can get the thing decorated and help keep 'em entertained that way. They were real upset over Freda, you know."

"Yes, I know. But they handled everything very well. Brenda's feeding them now." He sighed, resigned to the inevitable. "Yeah, you're right. I guess I'll get up in the attic and find those decorations."

"Fine. Then we'll be seeing you after a while."

"Tell Freda I'm really sorry about the accident. Tell her I'll be up to see her in the morning once I get the kids off to school."

Bret hung up and stared at the phone. A broken leg, at least. Maybe something even more serious. Why did something like this have to happen? It didn't make any sense.

None of it. Now Freda was in the hospital, suffering, and he was here at home trying to figure out what to do next.

The three older ones were in school during the day, at least until Christmas break. He would just have to take Travis around the ranch with him, or postpone his work until he could find someone to come in and look after the boy.

Who could he find, especially at this time of year? Everybody was busy with their own families.

He dropped his head into his hand and sat there at the desk, trying not to feel his weariness. He still had to get upstairs and find those blasted decorations, help the kids decorate the tree, give Travis his bath and make sure the girls got to bed at a decent hour.

"Oh, Patti," he whispered. "I need you so much."

As though aware of Bret's feelings, Rex padded into the office and rested his head on Bret's knee.

Bret straightened and looked down at the dog. "Did you come in here to comfort me?"

The dog thumped his tail.

"Freda's the one who needs some comforting, poor thing. The rest of us are doing just fine."

He wasn't at all sure Rex looked convinced, which wasn't surprising, since Bret didn't know exactly what he was going to do without a housekeeper.

He would just have to take it a day at a time rather than worry about a future over which he had no control. He pushed himself out of the chair and stroked Rex.

"C'mon, old man. We both need to get a move on. We've got a full evening ahead of us."

Bret headed toward the hall bathroom to wash up before finding out what Brenda had made them for supper.

As soon as supper was finished and the kitchen cleaned, Brenda offered to give Travis his bath while Bret found the decorations. Something had happened where his two oldest children were concerned, Bret realized as he pulled the ladder to the attic down from the ceiling and began to climb. Freda's accident had caused him to look at Chris and Brenda in a new light. Both of them had stepped in to help—Chris assisting Roy in getting Freda to the hospital and Brenda looking after the younger children.

They'd shown a surprising maturity that deeply touched him. Brenda was attempting to keep to a familiar routine in order not to alarm Sally and Travis any more than was absolutely necessary.

Bret knew that he could do no less. He was actually thankful to have the tree to trim, which should keep the children occupied until their bedtime.

Once he was in the attic, Bret mentally blessed Freda for keeping the storage area neat and orderly. The Christmas decorations were labeled and waiting in one of the corners. He carefully stacked the boxes and managed to get down both flights of stairs without mishap.

By the time the children came back downstairs from getting their baths and dressing for bed, he'd tested and strung the lights.

"We always have hot chocolate when we decorate the tree," Sally said pointedly. "Can we make some hot chocolate?"

"Uh, well—I'm not sure if we have the time to—"

"Don't worry about it, Dad," Brenda said. "I've got it ready to heat." She grinned at him, looking calm and in control of the situation. "I'll get it ready while you ride herd on these two."

He began to sort through the boxes, opening them and arranging them around the tree.

"Oh, Daddy, look!" he heard Sally say behind him. "Our angel! Isn't she beeootiful?"

Bret glanced down at the battered box that continued to hold the Christmas tree angel. Her dress no longer stood out quite so stiff and shiny. Her wavy hair could stand a good brushing, but her deep blue gaze was as potent as ever. He'd never before or since seen a doll with so much character in her face. The little angel remained a symbol for Bret of another lifetime…a time when he'd been young…a time when he'd actually believed in happy ever after.

He was glad Patti had insisted they keep their angel. She stirred bittersweet memories, but the memories were a part of who he was.

He watched Sally reverently lift the little angel from the box and carefully smooth her dress where it had been mussed from being packed away for the past year. Sally looked up and saw him watching her. She smiled and once again he saw Patti's smile in their daughter's face.

"Here, Daddy."

He took the angel even while he said, "Not yet, honey. Remember we put her on the tree the very last thing, after everything else is hung, just before we turn on the lights." He didn't point out to her that he'd already made sure all the lights were working first.

He glanced down at the angel in his hands. He couldn't seem to take his gaze away from her while the children quickly hung their treasures from Christmases past. He carefully smoothed wisps of hair away from her cheek before gathering the soft fluff of hair in his hand in an effort to subdue some of the curls.

She had such a wise look, as if she understood him and the pain that he perpetually carried in his heart. Bret knew he must be losing his wits to have such a strong reaction to a doll, even if she was supposed to be an angel!

He placed the angel on the mantel and turned to help Travis. Picking him up, Bret pointed out some of the higher branches that still needed decorating.

"Dad?" Brenda asked, carrying a tray with cups into the room and setting them down on the coffee table. "Did you find out how Freda's doing and when Chris is coming home?"

"Chris probably won't be home until late. He and Roy plan to wait at the hospital until the doctor finishes with all his tests."

"Was her leg broken?" Sally asked.

"'Fraid so, sugar," Bret replied.

"Well, who's supposed to look after us?" Sally asked. "What are we going to do without Freda?"

Bret readjusted Travis's weight on his hip, handed him a tiny rocking horse and waited while small hands arranged the ornament to a three-year-old's satisfaction before he answered. "It seems to me that we managed quite well last summer when Freda went to visit her sister for a few days, didn't we? None of you starved to death."

Brenda giggled. "Maybe so, Dad. But you really looked silly wrapped up in Freda's apron making pancakes."

Sally chimed in. "And you got real mad that time when you burned the biscuits you'd made for supper."

Bret forced himself to smile at the girls, recognizing their teasing was a way to lighten the atmosphere. "Okay, so maybe I need a little more practice. This will be a good time. According to the weather report, it's going to be too bad for me to work outdoors for the new few days, anyway." He looked down at his son who was still in his arms. "Travis and I'll find something to keep us busy, won't we, pardner?"

"Will Freda be here for Christmas?" Travis asked.

Since Travis seldom spoke they all looked at him in surprise.

Bret hugged his son a little closer to his chest. "I hope so, son, but it's too soon to tell just yet."

"School's out next Friday, Dad."

"I know, Brenda."

"Then we'll be here all day long for two weeks," Sally pointed out.

"I know."

There wasn't much to add to the conversation and for the next few minutes each of them concentrated on the tree.

Eventually, Brenda said in a subdued voice, "I wish we could go see Freda and let her know how much we miss her and how sorry we are she got hurt."

"Maybe we can, sweetheart," Bret replied. "I'll talk to the doctor tomorrow to see when he thinks she can have visitors." He glanced at the clock. "In the meantime, it's way past time for you to go to bed. School isn't out for the holidays yet."

"But Dad—"

"We have to—"

Brenda and Sally spoke at once, but it was Travis who was the most emphatic.

"You forgot the angel," he said with a great deal of indignation.

Bret stepped back from the tree and studied it. All the ornaments were hung…everything was in place…except for the angel.

"Sorry, gang," he muttered, leaning over and setting his pajama-clad son on the floor. He reached for the angel and carefully smoothed her dress and hair once more, then stepped on a nearby footstool so that he could reach the top of the tree.

With an ease from years of practice he attached the angel to the tree so that she faced the room. Then he climbed down from the footstool, walked over and turned off the overhead light, leaving the room in shadows. He returned to the tree and flipped on the switch.

The tree immediately came to life with a multitude of tiny lights flickering and twinkling among the scented branches.

"Oooh," Travis sighed softly. The girls took each of his hands and stared at the tree in awe.

Finally Brenda said, "I wish Chris could have been here. This is the first Christmas he hasn't helped us decorate the tree."

"I know, honey," Bret replied. "I miss him, too, but Roy says he was a real help today. At least he helped to choose the tree." He was silent for several moments, as they enjoyed the magical sight before them. His gaze returned to the angel who presided over the tree like a benevolent reigning monarch.

She'd been a part of this family for as long as there had been a family. Somehow having her with them once again gave him a sense of peace and a degree of normalcy to the unusual day. Nothing seemed quite as bad as before.

Brenda was the first to turn away, still holding Travis's hand. "You want me to put Travis to bed, Dad?"

"Thank you, honey, but Travis and I'll manage just fine, won't we?" Bret replied, smiling at his son. He held out his hand to Travis, who took it with a nod.

Spending time with Travis was always a pleasure to Bret. He enjoyed looking at the world through a three-year-old's eyes. The girls were patient with their little brother, but he didn't want them to feel overwhelmed with the responsibility of looking after him.

No matter how tired or sore Bret was each evening he made a point of spending the last hour of Travis's day with the boy.

His youngest scampered up the stairs, no

doubt racing ahead to find a story for Bret to read to him while the girls chattered about school as they left the room. Bret decided to leave the tree lights on for Chris when he came in. Roy would probably wait until morning to give him an updated report from the hospital. Bret knew he wouldn't sleep until he heard Chris come in, anyway.

By the time Bret heard Chris come up the stairs, Travis had fallen asleep—his giraffe tucked next to him.

Pausing in the doorway of his own room, Bret watched his oldest son come down the hallway toward him. Roy was right. Chris was growing fast, and not only in height. He was losing his boy-child look. His face appeared to be changing—his features looked sharper and more defined.

"How's it going, Dad?" he asked, following Bret into the room and sprawling out on the bed with a sigh.

Bret began to unbutton his shirt. "All right. How's Freda?"

"She was asleep when we left. The doctor gave her something for the pain. She's got a nasty sprain in her left ankle—probably caused when she tried to stop her fall—as well as a broken right leg. I was glad they gave her something. I could tell she was really hurting when we took her in, but she wouldn't complain.''

"Did the doctor have any idea when she'd be able to leave the hospital?''

"He wants to keep her at least a week, maybe longer. He said they may put her leg in traction because—'' He paused because Travis was trotting down the hallway toward them.

"I thought you were asleep,'' Bret said gruffly, shaking his head.

Travis ignored him and made a beeline for his brother. "The angel's here,'' Travis announced to Chris, crawling up on the bed beside him.

Chris glanced at Bret with a question in his eyes.

"We spent the evening decorating the tree,'' Bret explained.

Understanding flared in Chris's eyes. "Oh! So the angel's here, is she?'' he asked Travis, pulling him over to hug him. "Were you glad to see her?"

Travis nodded vigorously. "She always talks to me."

Chris's eyes met his dad's before he smiled at Travis and said, "I know, Travis. She used to talk to me, too."

Travis frowned. "Doesn't she talk to you anymore?"

Chris thought about that for a moment. "Good question. Maybe I haven't been listening as close as I used to," he admitted.

"C'mon, son," Bret said, picking Travis up and carrying him back to his bedroom. "It's way past your bedtime." He tucked him into bed once more, gave him a kiss and closed the door behind him.

He found Chris waiting for him in the hallway.

"What are we going to do now, Dad?"

"We'll manage somehow, son. I'll keep Travis with me. You and the girls are old enough to look after yourselves."

"I was really scared today. I mean, everything happened so fast. We heard Freda give a surprised cry, then we heard a big thump and pans clattering." He shook his head. "I was really glad Roy was here."

"Me, too. I'm also glad you were able to get the tree. At least it helped to keep the younger ones occupied tonight."

"Were you able to finish checking all the fences?"

"The worst ones, I think. The rest will have to wait." He patted his son's shoulder. "Things will work out. You'll see." He looked at his watch. "You're going to have a short night, son. Morning's going to come awful early for you."

Chris smiled at Bret, his eyes shadowed with concern. "I could stay home and help you if you'd like."

Bret shook his head. "We'll be fine, but I appreciate the offer. Good night, Chris," he said, turning away before Chris could glimpse the emotion he was feeling. His oldest son was no longer a child. He was rapidly becoming a fine young man. Wasn't it too soon? Did he have to grow up quite so fast?

Bret went back into his bedroom and finished undressing. Stripping out of his work clothes, he went into his bathroom for a shower. The hot spray felt wonderful to his sore muscles.

"You'd be proud of our children, Patti," he whispered, now that he was alone. "They handled today's emergency just fine."

He'd gotten in the habit of talking to Patti at times when his mind was in a turmoil. It seemed to help him sort through everything going on inside his head. He'd fill her in on his day, share with her his concerns about the ranch and the children.

Some folks would consider him crazy. They were probably right. But somehow he felt closer to her that way. By reviewing his day in this manner he sometimes saw solutions that he might have otherwise overlooked.

He was drying off when he remembered Travis's remark about the angel talking to him. Kids could say some of the most unexpected things. They must be born with a wild imagination.

All the children talked to Travis about his mother in an effort to make her real to the boy.

Bret had placed a framed photograph of Patti beside Travis's bed. He wasn't certain how much Travis understood what had happened to his mother. Bret hadn't wanted Travis to feel as though he were to blame for the loss of Patti. The doctor had been careful to explain to Bret and the three older children that her heart might have stopped whether she'd been in labor or not.

Bret reentered his bedroom and slipped on a clean pair of jeans. He zipped them, but didn't bother with the button since he was only going downstairs to make sure Chris had locked up when he came in. He'd forgotten to ask him if he'd looked in on the tree. Not that it mattered. Chris could always see it tomorrow. In the meanwhile Bret wanted to make certain the lights were turned off.

The house still retained the heat of the previous days' warm weather, although with this new cold front, he'd better make sure the thermostat on the furnace was set to come on.

Silently Bret made his way down the hallway, pausing only long enough to make certain the children were all in bed. Even Chris's light was out.

Bret went downstairs, found the back door locked and the thermostat set. He decided to set up the coffeepot, so that it would brew early in the morning. He'd have to get the children off to school before doing his regular chores. A fresh cup of coffee first thing would help to keep him going.

He paused in the doorway and gave the kitchen a last glance before he headed down the hallway to the living room. When he reached the doorway he came to an abrupt halt, staring at the figure in front of the fireplace with total disbelief.

A young woman stood on the braided rug, looking around the room with interest. From the light given off by the tree, he would guess her to be in her twenties. She was slim, with white-blond hair wrapped in a coil on her neck. She looked to be of average height and wore jeans, a plaid shirt and sensible low-heel shoes.

For a few moments he was too stunned to say anything. The woman hadn't noticed him. She was too busy studying the furnishings, running her hand along the polished wood of the mantel and delicately stroking the clock that sat there.

A sudden burst of anger shoved him into action. Bret flicked on the overhead light, its brightness almost blinding after the muted light from the tree. The woman spun around with a gasp, her hand going to her throat.

His smile was grim with satisfaction. Obviously he'd startled her as much as she had startled him.

"Who are you and how in blazes did you get in here?" he growled, not caring how intimidating he sounded.

She took a quick breath before she gave him a dazzling smile. "I'm Noelle."

Chapter Two

Noelle could feel her heart racing in her chest, which felt very strange to her. But then, at the moment everything felt strange.

She looked at Bret with a sense of uncertainty that she strove to hide, unsure about what she should say or do next.

He stood there staring at her in disbelief.

She couldn't blame him. She hadn't known exactly how to appear and it was now obvious that she hadn't quite worked out the finer points of her new role in the Bishop family's life.

Noelle had waited until they all went upstairs before she privately assumed human form. She was glad she'd waited. Finding herself inside a body adapted specifically for earth and gravity was quite a shock!

She had taken a couple of breaths, then released them and smiled. Air...she was taking in oxygen. Other sensations had captured her attention in a confusing array...sounds...and scents...and sights.

She had closed her eyes and waited for a sense of equilibrium. She'd thought she understood how human beings functioned, but she was rapidly adjusting all her perceptions now that her reality had changed so radically. She felt heavy—and more than a little sluggish—now that she had weight and substance.

She had stood before the twinkling Christmas tree and studied the small doll at the top. She could scarcely believe she used to exist in that tiny body. In comparison, she now felt like a giant...awkward and a little unsure of how to navigate her new body in a physical world.

Another unexpected gift was her heightened

awareness. She'd always thought she understood human senses...until now. Everything was so much...so much *more* than she had expected. She'd inhaled, taking in the intoxicating smell of fresh pine and scented candles. She could even smell a whiff of freshly baked breads and cookies from earlier in the day.

Not only her sense of smell had intensified. Lights and colors glittered and sparkled as though with a special life. She'd tilted her head with delight and listened to the ticking of the clock on the mantel and the gentle creaks of the house.

She'd been fascinated by her surroundings: the comfortably rumpled furniture, the wall hangings, the touches that made a dwelling a home for those who lived there. She had clasped her hands and sighed. Oh, this was going to be so much fun! She just knew that she and the family would—

That's when Bret had turned on the bright lights and interrupted her thoughts with his demand to know who she was and how she'd gotten inside.

His deep male voice had almost stopped her

heart from taking another beat! She stared at the man standing so belligerently in the doorway of the room.

Even if his words hadn't startled her, the overhead light would have. Its sudden brilliance almost blinded her with its glare.

Bret looked considerably different to her human eyes than her angelic ones. From her new perspective she could see that he was tall and very well built. Her conclusion was easy to reach since he wore very little clothing to hinder a thorough visual inspection of his body.

She found her reaction to him as startling as anything that had happened to her thus far. She couldn't seem to take her eyes off the broad expanse of his bare chest, which was covered with an intriguing design of soft curls. His arms and shoulders were strongly muscled and his hands, which rested on his hips near the low-slung waist of his jeans—his unbuttoned jeans—were well shaped and very capable looking. She could almost feel their callused roughness on her skin.

What a strange reaction!

Noelle blinked and tried to pull her attention back to his question. She smiled, hoping to soothe the anger she could feel washing toward her.

"I'm Noelle," she repeated, hoping to show him that she was no threat to him or his family, but he didn't appear to be reassured.

"That doesn't tell me a blasted thing! How did you get in here?" he demanded.

She gave a quick glance toward the tree before she said, "I knocked, but I guess nobody heard me, so I just came inside and waited." She looked out the window, shivering at the sound of the wind and steady rain.

"Like hell you did! The door was locked!"

She nodded. "Yes. I locked it when I came in."

He paused, thinking about her quiet explanation. Maybe Chris had forgotten to lock the door. Still—

"What are you doing here?"

She gave him another quick smile, feeling his anger easing slightly. "I was in town and heard what happened to Freda. I thought I would offer to fill in for her until she could return."

Noelle had an almost overpowering desire to assure him that she'd had nothing to do with Freda's accident, but of course he wouldn't understand. Perhaps later, when all the events unfolded, he would—

Before Bret could say anything more she asked, "How is Freda? Was she badly hurt?"

"Bad enough, but that's not the issue here. I've never seen you before. You're obviously not a local. How did you hear about the accident?"

This was the tough part. She had no experience with falsehoods. Then again, she couldn't very well explain to him who she was or why she was here. He'd have her hauled away and hospitalized. There was no help for it. Thankful that her supervisor had offered a plausible story, she said, "I'm from California. I came to visit my aunt, Ida Schulz. We were in town shopping today when we heard the news." She gave him her most innocent look. "Aunt Ida suggested I offer my services, so...here I am." Once again she smiled.

Ida Schulz lived on a remote ranch and rarely came to town. Noelle's supervisor felt that Ida was sufficiently removed from the scene not to be available to refute Noelle's story.

She waited for Bret's response. It wasn't long in coming.

"How did you get here? I didn't hear a car."

"One of Ida's hands drove me out here. Perhaps the storm muffled the sound of his truck. He waited until he saw me come into the house before he left."

As though finally becoming aware that he was still standing in the doorway, Bret walked fully into the room, coming to a halt a few feet in front of Noelle. Running his hand through his hair with frustration, he growled, "Look, I'm sorry you had to come all this way for nothing. You should have called first. We'll do just fine until Freda's better, so there's no need for you to..." His words slowed when he got a good look at her for the first time. "...fill...in." He stared at her in bemusement. He forgot what he'd been saying. He forgot everything but the presence of the woman standing little more than an arm's reach from him. Her eyes were a startling blue, but it wasn't the color that he found so mesmerizing. No. It was something else, something he couldn't define. There was a sense of familiarity, as though he'd looked into those eyes many times and had seen the wisdom there...the peace and the serenity.

He kept staring at her, feeling the same peace and serenity steal over him, so that he could feel his muscles relax, his body unwind, his mind cease its racing.

He lost track of time while he studied the woman before him until hc was jolted back into awareness once again by the sudden realization that he wasn't dressed. Feeling at a distinct disadvantage and blaming her for her unannounced entry into his home, he regained his emotional balance and control. He could feel his anger mounting once again. How dare this woman—this stranger!—come waltzing in here without notice and surprise a man in his own home. He felt like a fool standing there in his own home embarrassed because he wasn't wearing a shirt and socks.

"I don't understand any of this," he muttered, "and I don't like it. Nobody walks into a stranger's house like you've just done and offers to go to work." He crossed his arms over his bare chest. "I want to know what's going on and what you're doing here!"

"You don't believe me?" she asked faintly.

He stared at her for a long moment in silence, trying to decide what he believed. The woman looked young and innocent, wide-eyed and harmless.

Harmless? Not likely. A woman as attractive as she was couldn't be as naive as she was pretending to be. Bret groaned, running his hand through his hair, and took another step toward her.

She stood her ground, watching him.

Why, she wasn't afraid of him! How strange. She should be. After all, he towered over her, outweighed her by more than a hundred pounds. He could hurt her badly without even trying.

He stopped when he was a few inches from her. She had not moved. However, when she looked up at him, she blinked as though surprised to see the difference in their sizes.

Yeah, lady, he thought. *You'd better blink. And you'd better start using your head.*

"Look, whoever you are, I—"

"Noelle," she said in a quiet voice.

"Noelle," he repeated sharply. "I suppose I should thank you for—"

"Oh, you don't have to thank me! I'm delighted to be able to help you. I promise I won't be a bother. I can—"

"You don't understand. I can't have you stay here. It just wouldn't look right."

She stared up at him. "It wouldn't look right?" she repeated, puzzled.

"No! You're too young and too attractive to be staying here with—"

She burst into laughter. "Oh, that doesn't matter to me."

He couldn't take his eyes off her face. What was happening to him? How could he be so drawn to this strange young woman? How could he feel as though he knew her when he'd never seen her before in his life? He certainly wouldn't forget having met someone like her.

She took his hand and patted it gently for

all the world as though he were Rex. "It's going to be all right. You'll see."

Rex. Where was Rex and why hadn't he warned them of an intruder? He jerked his hand free and looked around for the dog. "Where's Rex? What did you do with him? Why didn't he—"

Responding to his name being called, Rex wandered into the room, yawning, as though he'd just been pulled out of deep sleep. He blinked bleary-eyed at Bret, silently questioning why his name had been mentioned.

Bret felt a momentary relief that the old dog was all right. "Some watchdog you are," he said gruffly, watching the animal amble toward him. "Why didn't you let me know she was here?"

Rex stopped and looked at Bret, then at Noelle. Slowly his tail began to wag. He gave a sharp *woof!* and trotted to her side, whining.

Bret watched in shock and amazement as Noelle knelt beside the dog and buried her head in his coat, her arms around him. "Hi, there, fella. It's good to see you. How're you doing?"

Bret couldn't believe what he was seeing. Rex was not a friendly dog. He was fiercely protective of the family and avoided everyone else. He tolerated Freda and Roy as though understanding the necessity for their being on the ranch but had little to do with them.

Bret had never seen Rex act this way before. He didn't know what to think.

Once again he ran his hand through his hair, wanting only to see the end of this rather harrowing day. "Look," he said, his voice echoing his irritation. "I don't know what's going on here but it's late...too late to drive you clear across the county to Ida's place. You can sleep in Freda's room tonight, okay? I'll figure a way to get you home tomorrow. Come on, I'll show you where Freda's room is located."

Bret spun on his heel and strode out the door, feeling as if he were in some strange dimension. Maybe this was another dream and he'd wake up soon to find himself in bed. Nothing made sense anymore.

He walked across the kitchen and opened a door, revealing a bedroom with its own small bath. He glanced over his shoulder and saw that Noelle had followed him, Rex staying close beside her.

Noelle peered around him at the neat room and its carefully made up bed. "This looks fine to me. Thank you."

He turned away, then paused and looked back at her. "Look," he said, "I'm sorry if I've been abrupt with you. It's just that I've had a rough day and finding you here so unexpectedly like that was a little unnerving."

"I understand."

"The thing is, we really don't need any help. I've managed on my own with the kids before. I can do it again. I appreciate your concern. Tell Ida I thank her for sending you, but it really wasn't necessary."

She touched him on the arm and once again he felt a strange peace settle over him. "Why don't you get some rest, Mr. Bishop. Things will look better in the morning. You need some sleep, that's all."

She had a point, one with which he was too tired to argue. He nodded and started across the kitchen. He paused in the doorway to the hallway and looked back. She stood watching him, Rex by her side.

"C'mon on, Rex. Go back to your bed," he called to the dog. Rex generally slept on the rug in Bret's office.

Rex just looked at him and blinked before he leaned against Noelle and sighed.

"I'll see that he goes to bed."

A strange woman comes into his house— God only knows how—and ends up sending him to bed with a promise to look after his dog?

Bret refused to think about it any longer. He was going to sleep.

Noelle let out a pent-up sigh of relief when she heard Bret's door close upstairs. He was really upset, something that she hadn't counted on when she'd made her plans.

Absently she patted Rex before turning and going into Freda's room.

Whether or not Bret wanted to admit it, Noelle knew she was needed here. The children needed her. So did their father.

Hadn't he realized how much he'd cut himself off from his emotions? It was only around the children that he allowed himself to feel anything. The rest of the time he locked himself behind a wall of indifference.

Well, at least she was here now. The first crucial step had been taken. She would have to face the next step tomorrow morning.

Noelle looked around the tidy room, wondering what she should do next. Her stomach growled, startling her. She rubbed the offending noisemaker with wonder. So this was what hunger felt like…as though she had an empty spot in her middle.

She understood empty spots, of course. Bret, whether he understood or not, was also hungry. He had lots of empty spots that needed to be filled. She hoped to make him aware of them between now and Christmas.

In the meantime, she might as well enjoy all that her new assignment had to offer. She went back to the kitchen to explore while Rex watched her.

She checked out the cupboards, the pantry and the refrigerator, sampling the different fare, fascinated by the different tastes. Being human was quite an experience, one she intended to fully explore.

After she ate, she tried out the shower in Freda's bathroom, another new sensation she

found exhilarating as well as surprisingly relaxing. After her shower she returned to the
bedroom and looked around her. She would
need some clothes.

No sooner had she thought of it than the
idea manifested itself in the form of a packed
suitcase that appeared open on the bed, with
clothes neatly folded inside.

"Thank you," she murmured absently,
searching for a· nightgown. Whoever had
packed for her had a strange sense of humor,
she decided, pulling out a nightshirt with Gar-
field on the front. She sat down at the dresser
and pulled the pins from her hair, then took
her time brushing out the long strands. After
dividing it into three parts and plaiting a single
braid, Noelle had started toward the bed when
she sensed a new presence in the room.

She glanced toward the door and smiled. A
tortoise-shell-colored cat sat watching her with
round, unblinking eyes. Noelle recognized her
immediately. Sally's cat was not supposed to
be in the house but whenever Sally thought
she could get away with smuggling her inside
without Bret's knowledge, she did so. Obviously tonight was no exception.

Noelle also knew that Rex detested the cat and that the feeling was mutual. She looked around and saw that Rex had fallen asleep on the rug beside her bed, looking as though he was down for the final count.

"Would you like to go outside, Mischief?" she whispered, waiting to see what the cat would do when she spotted Rex.

Mischief continued to stare at Noelle without blinking.

"Ah. You prefer the warm, dry house, do you?"

Mischief majestically stalked into the room and headed toward the bed. Rex roused, raising his head and eyeing his natural enemy. The two of them froze, their gazes locked in looks of unveiled hostility.

Noelle shook her head and sighed. "Oh, really, you two. We can't have this kind of behavior, you know. It really is time to learn some tolerance." She walked over and stroked each one of them, murmuring to them.

Eventually Rex lowered his head back on his paws and closed his eyes, while Mischief ignored his presence and leaped lightly onto the extra blanket folded at the foot of the bed. She turned around twice, then lay down in a furry ball, purring her approval.

"Yes, that's much better," Noelle said to them both before looking at Mischief. "Wouldn't you prefer to sleep with Sally?" she asked, sitting down beside the cat and lightly stroking her.

She paused, her fingers sensitively following the contours of the animal's body. "I see. Well, perhaps you're right in coming to me. I'll keep you safe."

With that Noelle turned out the light and slipped into bed.

The soft mattress felt wonderful. She hadn't realized how exhausting it was to manuever all this weight around. No wonder humans needed several hours of sleep each night. It felt wonderful to stretch and relax her muscles.

She sighed contentedly, feeling very pleased with herself. She'd done it. She was actually here snuggled down in bed, preparing herself for sleep. What fun!

Of course she still had some work to do where Bret was concerned. She'd known he was going to be a tough one to convince. Somewhere he'd gotten the idea that he had to do everything on his own without help.

She smiled sleepily to herself. He'd learn, oh, yes, he would. She was going to enjoy teaching him.

The next time Noelle opened her eyes she realized it was morning, although the sky had not lightened as yet. A soft whine and the thumping of a tail caught her attention.

"Good morning to you, too, Rex," she murmured. "Yes, I suppose it is time for us to be up, isn't it?" She wasted no time in getting out of bed and dressing, although for the moment she left her hair in the long braid. "Would you like to go outside?" she whispered.

Rex's tail whipped back and forth behind him. With a grin on her face she went into the kitchen, unlocked the door and let the German shepherd outside.

Noelle stood on the the porch and looked around. The storm from the evening before had passed, leaving a clear sky that was brightening as she watched. What a fascinating spectacle to see the stars begin to fade and warm color tint the eastern horizon.

With a smile on her lips she turned and went back into the house. Since it was too early for anyone to be awake, she took her time and explored all the downstairs rooms. Looking around she saw scuffed floors and battered furniture, tired decorations, abandoned toys and clothes that needed mending.

Poor Freda had had her hands full trying to keep up with everything and still have time to care for the family. She deserved her rest. Noelle was pleased to know that Freda's guardians were looking after her, helping her adjust to her change in circumstances.

She finished her inspection by returning to her room to make the bed and finish unpacking her clothes. She found Mischief in the closet.

"Ah, so there you are. I see you fared well during the night, my friend." She touched the soft fur behind the cat's ear and rubbed gently. "You picked a safe, quiet place and I won't disturb you."

Leaving the door to the closet partially

opened, she turned away, wondering how Bret was going to deal with his next decision. Yes, he certainly had his hands full.

She returned to the kitchen, discovered the coffee was ready to brew, turned the machine on and decided to start breakfast, knowing the family would be getting up before much longer.

The biscuits were in the oven and the bacon was frying on the stove when she heard someone on the stairs. She turned and waited for her first visitor.

Travis appeared in the kitchen doorway rubbing his eyes. His hair was tousled, his pajamas rumpled and his slippers were on the wrong feet. He clutched a rather battered-looking stuffed giraffe.

"Good morning, Travis. You're up early."

Still half asleep, he started toward her. "I smelled something good cooking and it woke me up. I was—" He realized for the first time that Noelle wasn't Freda. His eyes seemed to grow in his face. She removed the bacon, wrapping it in absorbent paper towels, then went over to the table and sat down.

Travis still stood frozen in the middle of the floor.

She smiled at him and held out her hand.

Slowly, like a sleepwalker, he moved toward her. "It's you," he breathed in awe.

"Yes."

"I di'nt know you was real."

"I am."

He stopped when he reached her side. "Can I touch you?"

"Yes, you may."

He stuck out his forefinger and carefully placed it on her denim-clad knee. "W-w-o-o-w-w," he whispered. "You *are* real, you really and truly are." He reached up and touched her braid, stroking it. "I like your hair better hanging loose."

"I wear it that way when I'm all dressed up, but when I'm working around the house, I need it out of my way."

He walked around her. "Where are your wings—and your halo?"

"I only wear those for formal occasions as well."

"Oh."

He came around in front of her again. "Do you have a name?"

"It's Noelle."

"Noelle," he repeated, his lips curving. "That's a pretty name."

"Thank you."

He leaned his elbow on her knee and casually crossed one foot over the other. "Do you know my mother?"

Tenderly she brushed his silky hair off of his face. "Yes, Travis, I do. She's a very special lady."

"She's an angel, too, you know," he confided.

"Is she?"

"Uh-huh. My daddy told me. Is she going to come see us, too?"

Noelle swallowed. "No, Travis. I'm afraid not."

He straightened, patting her knee. "It's okay. I know she's pretty busy. I never knew her," he added matter-of-factly, "so I thought maybe I could see her."

"She visits you whenever she can, mostly when you sleep."

He grinned. "An' Chris and Brenda and Sally, too?"

"Them, too," she agreed.

"And Dad? He really misses her, I think. Sometimes when he's in my room he stares at my picture of her and looks sad."

She could think of nothing to say to that, so instead she asked, "Are you ready to eat?"

"Mmm, yes," he replied, rubbing his stomach.

"Would you like some oatmeal, or an egg or—?"

He looked at the biscuits. "One of those, and some bacon and I guess an egg."

She leaned over and hugged him. "Coming right up," she said, getting up and going to the refrigerator.

"Are you going to take care of us until Freda comes back?"

"I'll be here for a little while, yes."

"That's good." He climbed up into his chair and watched her, his arms folded around his giraffe.

"What's your giraffe's name?"

"Harvey."

"Oh. Did you name him?"

"Uh-uh. My daddy gave him to me a long, long time ago."

"So your dad named him."

"Nope. Harvey named hisself. He jus' tole me it."

"Oh, of course. Silly of me to forget we pick our own names."

"Yeah, only I forgot about picking mine. They had to teached it to me again when I could finally remember."

Noelle placed his breakfast in front of Travis and sat down across from him to eat her own in companionable silence. They heard a door open upstairs, another door close, a shower come on, and one of the girl's voices.

Travis looked over at Noelle, his eyes sparkling. "Boy! Are they going to be surprised to find you here!" He finished his milk and slid down out of his chair. "I'm going to go tell 'em," he said, racing off.

The family members would be down shortly. She'd better get the rest of their breakfast ready for them. She was sorry Patti wasn't there, too. For a brief moment of longing, she wished her stay wasn't going to be so short.

She was here now, she reminded herself, and she definitely had her work cut out for her.

She cleared the table of her dishes and went back to fixing breakfast.

Bret smelled the fresh coffee, frying bacon, warm biscuits and smiled in his sleep. All of it smelled so good, especially the coffee. He wanted a cup...but not enough to let go of the woman he held in his arms. The swaying rustle of palm trees and the gentle swish of nearby water added to the sense of paradise he'd found in her arms. He stroked his hand over her hair, feeling the silkiness ripple beneath his palm as he smoothed his hand over her shoulder, lingered, then moved down until he could cup her breast.

She sighed and he could feel her lips brush against his mouth just as he—

"Dad? Aren't you up yet?" Chris's adolescent voice jolted Bret into immediate wakefulness. Wild-eyed he stared around him in alarm, relieved to discover that his son hadn't caught him on a beach with a blond-haired, haunting blue-eyed woman in his arms.

It was a dream, that's all it was. He'd just been dreaming about...about...a face popped into his mind and he groaned.

"Dad?" His door swung open.

Bret jerked up in bed, trying to look awake. "Yeah, I'm here. Guess I must've forgotten to set my alarm."

Chris looked at his dad, then back over his shoulder. "Well, if you're still in bed, who's downstairs making breakfast?"

Now that the door was open the aroma of coffee wafted in even stronger, along with the smell of biscuits and bacon, causing his mouth to water.

Bret yawned. "How'd you know it wasn't me?"

"Because your door was still closed. It's always open unless you're asleep," he absently explained. "So what's going on? Who's downstairs?"

"Ida Schulz's niece arrived late last night. Said she'd heard about Freda and offered to help out for a few days."

"No kidding? Ida Schulz? I never knew she had a niece."

"Neither did I. Guess you learn something new every day."

"So how old is she? Is she good-looking?" Chris turned away as though to take a peek.

Bret grinned. "Too old for you, buddy. Since when have you been so interested in what a woman looks like?"

His son shot him a purely masculine expression that spoke volumes. "See you downstairs, Dad," he finally said with a lopsided grin before he turned around and disappeared down the hall.

Bret was shaving when he heard Travis calling him. "Daddy! Daddy, where are you?"

"In here, son," he said. "What's the matter?" He leaned around the door into the bedroom in time to see his youngest child bolt around the corner, his eyes sparkling with excitement.

"Did you see her, Daddy? Did you see? It's the angel! She's come to look after us. She's never done that before!"

Bret paused in his shaving. "The angel?"

Travis bobbed his head vigorously. "Our angel. You know. She's in our kitchen and—"

"Oh! You must be talking about Noelle." He knelt beside his pajama-clad son. "Honey, Noelle isn't an angel, although I suppose her showing up at such a time could be considered a godsend."

"Oh, yes, she is. She tol' me so." Travis's bottom lip edged out belligerently.

"She must not have understood what—"

"Daddy!" Sally cried, sounding distraught. She came running into the bedroom and came to a skidding halt beside Travis in the bathroom doorway, her hair standing in uncombed peaks all over her head. "Daddy! I can't find Mischief anywhere! Have you seen her?"

Bret straightened to his full height and frowned down at his daughter. "Are you telling me that you let Mischief in the house when you know she isn't supposed to be in here?"

"I *had* to let her in last night," she replied, dramatically. "It was wet and cold outside and she had nowhere to sleep—"

"Except in the warm barn curled up in the soft hay," he reminded her sternly.

Sally's shoulders drooped. "But, Daddy, something's wrong with her. I couldn't get her to eat last night and she kept pacing back and forth, crying. I couldn't throw her out in the cold. She seemed a little better when I put her in my room, but when I woke up this morning, she was gone! Do you think she's died?'' Her large gray eyes stared up at him, desolate.

How did they learn how to do that at such an early age? Bret wondered.

''I doubt very much if she died, Sally. Mischief looked perfectly healthy the last time I saw her. Have you checked everywhere downstairs?''

''Downstairs? Oh, she wouldn't go downstairs. She hates Rex, remember?''

''I don't know what to tell you, Sally, except that you need to go eat so you won't be late for school.''

Sally walked away, carrying the weight of the world on her delicate shoulders.

Bret turned back to Travis. ''C'mon, sport. We need to get you dressed. From the looks of that pajama top, you've already had your breakfast.''

Travis smiled sweetly at his father. ''Noelle's a real good cooker, Daddy.''

"I'm glad to hear it, son," he said. "Let me finish shaving and I'll be in your room in a few minutes to help you dress."

When Bret walked into the kitchen Noelle was the only one there. "Mornin'," he muttered to the woman standing at the stove, her back to him. He strode over to the counter and poured himself a cup of coffee.

She turned around, smiling at him. "Good morning," she replied, and carried a plate of perfectly basted eggs to the table and set it at his place. "Help yourself to the bacon and biscuits."

He couldn't resist taking a sip of the savory coffee before he cleared his throat and said, "Look, you didn't have to make breakfast this morning. I'm perfectly capable of looking after this family. I just happened to oversleep this morning. Otherwise I would have—"

"Oh, but I've enjoyed it. This is what I came to do, to help out wherever I'm needed." She looked past his shoulder and smiled. "Good morning."

Bret heard Chris say, "Mornin'," his voice cracking slightly, before he circled the table and sat down across from him. Bret noted that his son—who normally paid no attention to what he looked like—had carefully combed his hair and put on a freshly ironed shirt. When Chris's gaze met his father's, Bret lifted his brow slightly and watched his eldest child blush a fiery red.

Bret had almost finished his breakfast when he was interrupted by a wail coming from Sally in another room. "Daddy, I can't find her *anywhere!*"

He glanced around in time to see the tragic face of his youngest daughter, still in her pajamas, having gone nowhere near a hairbrush since his last glimpse of her.

"Sally, go get dressed or you're going to be late for school. The cat will show up sooner or later, you can depend on it. She's a survivor and she knows how to take care of herself."

"The cat?" Noelle repeated. "Are you looking for your cat?" Everyone looked around at her in surprise. She grinned and silently motioned Sally to follow her into Freda's room. Chris immediately followed. Reluctantly, Bret shoved his chair back and joined the parade.

From the doorway he watched Noelle tiptoe to the closet and widen the opening. There, on a couple of blankets lay Mischief with four tiny lumps of fur beside her, none of them the same color. When it came to romance, Mischief obviously lived up to her name.

Sally fell on her knees in front of the cat. "Oh, Mischief, look at you! A Christmas present for each one of us. Aren't you the sweetest thing?"

The cat arched her neck so that Sally could scratch her behind her ear in the prescribed manner while Bret attempted damage control. "Now wait just a minute, Sally. Four more cats around here are the very last things we need."

Chris peered over Sally's shoulder and grinned. "Look at that one. All black except for white-tipped toes. I'll call it Lucifer."

"I want the striped one. It looks like a ferocious tiger, doesn't it, Chris?" Sally whispered. "That's what I'll call it. Tiger."

"What 'cha looking at?" Travis wanted to know, pushing past his dad into the room.

Bret sighed, knowing when he was on the losing side of an argument.

"Kitties!" Travis exclaimed, dashing to get a closer look.

"Shh!" Sally and Chris echoed.

"Don't scare 'em," Chris went on. "Or she'll move 'em somewhere else and we won't be able to find them."

"Heaven forbid," Bret grumbled. He happened to glance at Noelle and saw a sympathetic look in her eyes. He turned and went back for another fortifying cup of coffee. Unfortunately for his digestion, he could still hear the conversation in the other room.

"The tiger-striped one is mine," Sally was explaining to her awestruck little brother, "and the black one is Chris's. Which one of the other two do you want?"

Normally Bret was a logical man. He considered himself totally rational. But the past several hours had been far from normal and for a brief moment he actually found himself blaming Noelle for the fact that Mischief had decided to present the family with four kittens just before Christmas.

Being—on the whole—a fair person, Bret admitted to himself that Noelle could certainly cook up a mean bunch of biscuits. What she had done with the eggs and bacon was almost mystical. He forced himself to be fair. Noelle was no more to blame for Freda's fall than she was for those blasted kittens.

The children chattered over their breakfast, filling in all the exciting details to Brenda when she arrived downstairs.

Bret noticed that all of them were chatting with Noelle as though they were old friends. Children continued to amaze him. They had taken her presence in stride, adapting to a new order of things without a grumble. They were already gathering up their books, putting on their coats, getting ready to leave, the whole time chatting with Noelle as though she'd always been a part of their family circle.

Not that their attitudes made any difference to the outcome of the situation.

She could not stay and that was the end of it. Just as soon as the older ones left for school he would set her straight. He would—

Travis walked over to Noelle and said, "I hope you're going to stay with us for a long, long time."

Bret and the children stared with varying degrees of disbelief. Travis was quiet. Travis took a long time to warm up to people. Even with people he knew, Travis was aloof. Seeing his son with his arms entwined around the woman who Bret had fully intended to send away shook him. What was going on here? How had she managed to bewitch his son?

"Are you going to tell me some more stories? Will we get to—"

"Travis?"

Travis looked around at his father.

"I'm afraid you must have confused Noelle with someone else. I don't believe you know—"

"Yep, I do!" His son nodded with emphasis, then reluctantly let go of Noelle's waist. "She's the angel."

Chris paused in shoving his foot into his boot. "The what?"

Big people could certainly act dumb, sometimes. Travis put his hands on his hips, unconsciously mimicking one of his father's habitual poses, and said in a very patient voice, "She's the angel...you know." He waved his arm toward the living room. "She comes to visit every year!" He spun back to her. "But I like you best when you're just like real people." He threw his arms around her again in a big bear hug.

Bret shook his head, dumbfounded. Not so his vocal children.

"Wow! Travis is right. She *does* look like the Christmas angel," Chris said in awe.

"I knew you looked familiar!" Brenda exclaimed.

"Wait until I tell my friends," Sally added, her eyes wide.

"Whoa, whoa, wait a minute." Bret finally found his voice. "I don't care who she looks like, or who she reminds you of, this is Noelle, Ida Schulz's niece." He glared at his younger daughter. "If you go spouting to your friends that an angel cooked your breakfast, they're going to have you taking all kinds of mental tests."

Noelle hadn't said anything. Now she leaned down and whispered something in Travis's ear. He nodded, relaxed his hold on her and scampered out of the room.

Chris broke the silence. "We've gotta go. The bus will be here shortly." He turned to Noelle. "Thanks for breakfast. It was great."

Travis returned with one of his small trucks and perched on one of the chairs. Bret tried to think of something to say. His son looked very content. Was there really a good reason to drag him outside in the cold when he could stay here with Noelle? He knew he didn't want her here, but he had to look at the larger picture. He had to decide what was best for Travis, as well.

He wished he knew what to do. He wished he knew what to say. Since she hadn't sat down since he came downstairs, he asked, "Aren't you going to eat?"

Noelle chuckled. "I already ate. There's something about the air this time of year that's given me quite an appetite."

"I didn't know angels got hungry," Travis said.

Noelle acted as though his comment was perfectly natural. She didn't smirk or smile in a patronizing way. Bret appreciated her tact. He wouldn't have wanted her to hurt Travis's feelings. Instead, she slid into one of the vacated chairs and propped her chin on her palm. "Normally angels don't get hungry," she admitted. "It depends on what they have to do and where they're working."

Travis nodded very seriously. "I'm glad you've come to work here. We can have lots and lots of talks, just like before, right?"

Bret had never seen such a loving smile on anyone's face when Noelle nodded, and said, "I'm glad to be here. We'll have some wonderful talks while I'm here."

Yes, she had neatly cut the ground right out from under him. If he sent her away now, Travis would be upset. Why had she encouraged his son to think she was some kind of angel, anyway? Granted, he could see a resemblance between her and the angel at the top of their Christmas tree...the same color eyes and hair, the same slender build. But this woman was far from an angel! She knew exactly what she was doing when she flashed those eyes so provocatively at him, the way she was now.

"More coffee?" she asked.

Right. That may be what she said, but it

wasn't what she was thinking. Why, every time she looked at him, he felt the jolt all the way down to his toes. "No. I've got work to do." He walked over and put on his coat. He grabbed his hat and pulled the brim down low over his eyes.

Deciding to put his son to the test, he looked over at Travis. "Do you want to come help me with my chores today, son? I could use some extra hands feeding the animals."

"Could Noelle come, too?" Travis asked, his eyes shining.

"Well, I don't think—"

"I'd love to!" she said. "I haven't had a chance to be around animals for…oh, a long, long time." She met Bret's glance with equally shining eyes.

Well, that little experiment certainly blew up in his face. Why did he feel like such a grouch? What possible difference did it make to him whether she stayed or not?

Silly question.

He didn't want to be reminded of her or the dreams he'd had about her all night. Having her stay here at the ranch would be too much of a strain. She meant well, no doubt, but she just didn't understand that—

"I'll clean the breakfast dishes and be ready to go whenever you are."

Travis scooted out of his chair and darted out into the hallway, his footsteps echoing on the stairs. "I left my coat upstairs," he called. "I'll be right back."

Bret looked at Noelle, once again feeling powerless over the events around him. He pulled off his hat and began to turn it between his fingers. "Look, I—uh—"

"Oh, please don't thank me. I want to thank *you* for the opportunity to be with you and your family for the next few days. It's literally a dream come true for me. I feel very blessed."

"I'm sure you find it strange that Travis thinks you're the Christmas angel. The thing is, that, well—he's—"

"He's wonderful! Bright, full of life and so very innocent. He's delightful and you must be very proud of him."

Bret absently studied his mangled hat through sightless eyes. "Yeah, I am." He forced himself to meet her gaze. "His mother died when he was born. He was like a miracle God gave me when He took Patti. None of us in the family would have been the same without Travis."

"I'll watch over him very carefully, Mr. Bishop."

The title caught him off guard, reminding him that she had called him that last night. Nobody called him Mr. Once again she'd managed to make him feel uncomfortable. He didn't like the feeling. Not at all.

"My name is Bret," he muttered, hearing the ungracious tone and not being able to do a blasted thing about it. He knew he was telling her more than his first name. He was also agreeing that she could stay at the ranch with him and the children until Freda could return.

He knew he was making a big mistake. He just didn't know how to get out of it. He felt as though fate had jockeyed him into some kind of corner where he couldn't get out. He didn't know exactly how it had happened and he was bewildered by the whole sequence of events.

When she didn't say anything in response, he turned toward the hallway. "I'll go help Travis find his coat. We'll be down in a few minutes."

"Bret?" she said to his back.

He stiffened, feeling his name on her tongue like a caress down his spine. He forced himself to turn around and face her. "Yes?"

"It's going to be okay. I promise."

"I'm sure you really believe that, but I don't agree with you. Human nature being what it is and all, I think we're both making a big mistake here. If we were smart, we'd make up some excuse why you can't stay."

She looked startled. "Human nature?" she echoed, wonder in her voice.

Impatient, he said, "Yeah! Human nature. You know. Man. Woman. Male. Female. Birds. Bees. All that kind of stuff. I'm a normal red-blooded American male, lady, with my fair share of needs. I've managed to handle my situation because I've kept myself too busy to give it much thought. Plus I haven't allowed myself to spend much time with any women that might remind me of what I've been missing. You moving in here is going to change all of that.''

If anything, her eyes grew lovelier as they continued to stare at him. ''Are you saying that you're attracted to me?''

She sounded absolutely astonished, which ticked him off something terrible. ''What's the matter with you, don't you ever look in a mirror? Of course I'm attracted to you! I'm not dead, dammit! I thought all those feelings died along with Patti and I'm telling you the truth, I'm not at all happy about finding out they're still alive and kicking, rarin' to go!''

Noelle became very still, as though she were listening to something only she could hear. The echo of *his* voice still rang in the room and once again he felt foolish to have made such an outburst in front of this woman.

What was it about her that made him so uncomfortably self-conscious?

He spun away and started toward the hallway once again.

''I'm attracted to you, as well,'' she said softly, which effectively stopped him in his tracks. In fact, he felt paralyzed. Was she out of her mind, making such an admission? He forced himself to face her once more.

"Hasn't anyone ever warned you that it's dangerous to be too honest?" he growled.

"No."

"Then let me be the first."

"I shouldn't have told you how I feel?"

"You got that right."

"Even if it's the truth?"

"Especially if it's the truth!"

"I don't understand."

He shoved his hand through his hair, feeling his blood pressure mount. "Where have you spent your life, in a convent?"

She smiled. "Close."

"Well, then you'd better smarten up fast, or some guy's going to come along and take advantage of all that sweet innocence of yours."

"You wouldn't."

"I'm not the only guy around."

She smiled. "But you'll protect me from those others, so I'm safe enough."

"Maybe so, but who's going to protect you from me?" Once again she looked puzzled. Bret muttered beneath his breath, then shook his head. How could he explain something he couldn't fully understand himself? "Forget it. I've got to go help Travis."

He was already in the hallway when he distinctly heard her say in a voice just above a whisper, "I enjoyed our time on the beach together, Bret Bishop."

A wave of dizziness swept over him. How could the woman possibly have known about his dream?

Chapter Three

"I understand Ida Schulz's niece is helping you at home these days," Freda said. "How is she working out for you?"

Bret had just arrived at the hospital a few minutes before. Rather than give an immediate answer, he looked around the room, then walked over to one of the chairs. Settling into its depths, he stretched his long legs in front of him, crossing his ankles with a sigh. "Okay, I guess," he muttered, staring at the toes of his scuffed boots.

"Now there's some real enthusiasm for

you," she said after a moment, when she realized he wasn't going to volunteer anything more. "What's the matter, afraid I'll get my feelings hurt to hear how well she's taking care of everything?"

He glanced up at her. "I miss you, Freda."

"I miss you, too, Bret. And I miss the kids."

"Life was a lot less complicated when you were at home with us."

She shifted slightly, trying to find a comfortable position. After four days in that infernal bed, she was ready to get out of there. "What's causing you problems now?"

He lifted his shoulders in a shrug. "I don't know how to describe it exactly. Things are different these days. Noelle seems to have taken over."

"And you resent that?"

"Not exactly. I'm just puzzled by it all." He glanced up, giving her a halfhearted smile. "Travis insists she's our Christmas tree angel come to life."

"Yes. He was all excited about her visit when Roy brought them in yesterday." She eyed his pensive expression and said, ''I don't see any harm in his believing she's an angel, do you, Bret?''

As though he could no longer sit still, Bret straightened and leaned his elbows on his knees, staring at the floor between them. ''At this point, I'm too confused to know what to think,'' he finally said. He looked up at her, his pain evident. ''When Patti died, I wanted to die, too. If I hadn't had the children I wouldn't have made it through these last few years. Even with the children, I've been too busy to think about anything but getting through each day.''

''And now?''

''Now all I seem to think about is a slip of a girl who seems to have wrapped my kids in some kind of magical cloak. They seem so happy these days. They don't argue as much, they're so helpful around the place, I'm constantly amazed.''

Freda started laughing.

''What's so funny?''

''Well, I would say that you're finally waking up and noticing the world around you.''

"What's that supposed to mean?"

"It's Christmastime, Bret. The children have always behaved themselves around Christmas, hoping that their behavior will encourage you to get everything on their list."

"You think that's all this is?"

"What I think is that in the past you've kept yourself aloof from Christmas. You've let me take the kids shopping, you've had Roy pick up the special gifts they find under the tree. You did everything you could to ignore the whole business."

"I guess that was a lot to ask of you and Roy."

"That's not my point. My point is that you've encased your feelings in some kind of deep freeze...until now."

"You think so?"

"Oh, yes. I see a definite thawing going on." She smiled. "Chris says Noelle is one awesome babe."

Bret blinked. "Awesome babe? What's that supposed to mean?"

"I took it to mean he's impressed with her looks."

He fidgeted a moment before saying, "The kid's got good taste."

"Definitely thawing, I would say," she murmured. "It's time you let Patti go, Bret. She wouldn't have wanted to see you like this, all grim and uptight about everything. What I remember about Patti is how she could always get you to see the humor in every situation. One of your problems recently is that you take life too seriously."

He met her gaze without smiling. "Life *is* serious, Freda."

"Actually, life is too *important* to be taken seriously, Bret. Life is meant to be enjoyed…each and every moment. I believe the reason Noelle has come into your life…and the children's lives…is to remind you of how much life has to offer, to shake you out of your rut, to make you look at your life."

"Noelle came into our lives because Ida Schulz told her to come help us out after you fell."

"Ah, Bret. Must you be so literal?"

"Well, I certainly don't see her visit as some kind of miracle. I'll admit that it was a help to me that she happened to be visiting from California, and that she heard about—''

''God works in mysterious ways, his wonders to perform.''

He raised a brow. ''You think God sent her?''

''I wouldn't be at all surprised.''

''Well, if that's the case, I'm in deep trouble because I've been having some unheavenly reactions to her.''

''No doubt you're reacting like a normal, red-blooded human being who's been living too long without a companion. It's all right to admit that you get lonely, you know.''

''I haven't had time to think about it.''

''You haven't *wanted* to think about it, which is why you've kept yourself so busy, burying yourself out on that ranch and refusing to take part in anything.''

''So what do you think I should do?''

''Join in the celebration of Christmas. Be a part of it all. Allow yourself to feel again, to believe again.''

He shook his head. ''I'm not a kid any longer, Freda.''

"Sometimes I wonder if the children aren't the wise ones. They accept—with gratitude and without questioning—all the good things in life. Perhaps we could learn from their example."

"I'm surprised you can say that considering that you're lying here in a hospital with a broken leg."

She smiled. "I'm here to tell you that it's been downright good for me. I've discovered several things about myself and my life while I've been forced to lie here. It isn't so bad to take time out to reflect about life. I found that I'm not indispensable. You and the children have been doing quite well without me. I discovered that I'm enjoying having some time to myself where I can catch up on my reading and such." She watched him closely as she said, "You know, my sister still wants me to go to Austin when I get out of here."

"You were planning to spend Christmas with her, anyway. Does the doctor think you can be released by then?"

"Oh, I think so. He's pleased with my progress. I've got to learn to get around on crutches first, and I can't do that until my sprained ankle gets a little better.''

"You're certainly cheerful about the whole thing.''

She smiled, her eyes twinkling. "I always believe that things work out the way they're supposed to. I already see a lot of good coming out of my accident.''

"If you say so.''

"Think about taking the kids Christmas shopping, Bret. Get out there with them and look at everything. Listen to the music, watch the people, catch the holiday spirit.''

"Hah! Now that *would* be a miracle.''

"I happen to believe in them, myself.''

He got up and leaned over the bed, hugging her. "Thanks for the pep talk, Freda. I appreciate your comments and concern.''

"You're going to do just fine, Bret. I know you will.''

"Wish I had your faith.''

"Eventually you probably will.''

On the drive home Bret thought about his conversation with Freda. Perhaps she was right about his having put his emotions in a deep freeze. He loved his kids but he wasn't sure how much he showed them his love. He couldn't remember the last time he'd done anything with them, just for fun.

He hadn't realized how self-absorbed he'd been, totally wrapped up in his own misery.

The first thing that had happened to him after Noelle's arrival was the realization that he wasn't a eunuch! The dream he'd had the first night had certainly made that fact clear. He'd had trouble looking at her for the rest of the day without being reminded of all that his subconscious had him doing with her.

He hadn't had the courage to ask her what she'd meant about enjoying their time on the beach together. Had he had some kind of mental lapse and actually told her? He shook his head, wishing he understood what was going on at his house these days.

Like it or not, he found himself working closer around the house, stopping more often to check on Travis, even though he quickly learned how much Travis enjoyed his new friend.

Then there were those times when he'd

catch her looking at him and their gazes would lock until he felt as though he was going to drown in those deep blue eyes. Somehow she made him feel as though he had no secrets from her. Normally he would be upset to think he was so easily read and understood, but with Noelle, he almost felt a sense of relief.

He drove into the ranch and followed the lane to the house, reminding himself to call Ida Schulz and thank her for sending Noelle to them.

At dusk the house looked like something on a calendar, or maybe a Christmas card. The building itself was a mellowed gray and the bright glow of golden color from the downstairs windows beckoned any weary traveler to come inside and find comfort. He wasn't certain what it was about the house that made it so different. He couldn't believe that Noelle's presence could contribute to the overall restful quality but he couldn't deny noticing some of the changes.

In the four days she'd been there he could see the effect she'd had on the children. There seemed to be more laughter in the house since she came. Travis had turned into a chatterbox, giggling and repeating stories she'd told him.

And what stories! He'd never before heard of such a powerful imagination as this woman had. She admitted that she seldom watched television and he guessed he'd have to accept that since he'd never seen any program to match her tales.

In addition to the changes he'd seen in the children, he'd also noticed that the house appeared brighter...almost newer, especially the old linoleum in the kitchen. When he'd mentioned the difference, Noelle explained that she had found a new cleansing agent that brought back the original color and shine to the old covering.

The oak floors in the rest of the house looked as if they'd been refinished and buffed so fine he could almost see his reflection in them, causing the thick area rugs to look like colorful islands floating on a polished sea.

The sofa in the living room had lost its sagging appearance, and new throw pillows had added bright color to the room.

Whenever he commented on some change,

Noelle made light of her efforts, so he hadn't bothered to mention that his clothes had never looked brighter or cleaner. He either found them neatly folded in his drawers or hanging with precision and precise pleats in his closet.

Bret stepped up on the back porch and let himself into the kitchen. As usual, the room was spotless and gleaming, but he could still smell the savory remains of supper. She'd set large helpings aside, no doubt for him, and he intended to eat every bite as soon as he washed up.

He paused in the hallway because he heard Noelle's voice. It sounded as though she was in the middle of one of her stirring sagas. Without giving his actions much thought, Bret sank onto the bottom step of the stairway to listen.

"...so when the train started up the steep grade the engine had trouble pulling all that weight up the hill, which meant the train was forced to go slower and slower," she was saying.

"I know, I know," Sally interrupted, obviously excited. "That's how that mean ol' robber could jump on, isn't it? He didn't have to make the driver—''

''The engineer—'' Chris interjected smoothly.

''Yeah—the engineer—slow down, 'cause he could get on without anybody noticing.''

''But wouldn't one of the train guards see him?'' Brenda asked.

''Maybe he made himself invisible,'' Travis suggested gravely.

''Oh, Travis,'' Sally began, ''People can't—''

''Shh! Let Noelle go on,'' Brenda snapped.

Silence reigned for a telling moment before Noelle continued.

''The robber knew exactly where the guards were stationed. He waited until the perfect moment to leave the boulders he'd used for cover and raced toward the train. He leaped for the train and grabbed on to one of the metal steps that led to the top of the baggage car. He scrambled to get his feet on another one so that he could—''

''Are you trying to glamorize the profession of train robbery, by any chance?'' Bret interrupted from where he now stood, leaning against the doorjamb, his arms folded across his chest.

"Daddy, you're home!" Sally announced.

"Hey, Dad, did you see Freda?" Chris asked.

"Dad, Noelle said you might take us shopping tomorrow," Brenda said, catching him off guard. How had Noelle known that he'd considered going this year? Brenda was still talking. "I told her that you usually had Roy or Freda take us but she said to ask you, anyway. Will you?"

Travis grabbed him around the knees and said, "Don't you want to hear about what happened to the train robber?"

He looked over the children's heads to where Noelle sat in the middle of the sofa. The children had been clustered around her, listening intently. A small fire danced in the fireplace, giving off a rosy glow.

The most surprising addition was Rex stretched out asleep in front of the fire while Mischief sat nearby, ignoring his presence while she fastidiously groomed herself.

He'd found a very domestic scene, one that was rarely enacted in this house. Somehow this woman had managed to captivate all four of the children with her tale, a tough job with such a wide range of ages.

"How was the last day of school?" he asked, hoping to buy himself some time before facing all their questions.

Brenda beamed. "Oh, Dad, I aced my test this morning. You know, I didn't really understand the theory behind the equations. I felt like such a dunce because the teacher had explained it over and over, but somehow it just didn't make sense to me. When I showed Noelle my homework she immediately saw where I was confused." Brenda glanced at Noelle. "Somehow she explained it in a way that made the whole thing seem so simple. I was trying to make something hard out of it!" She laughed. "Even the teacher was surprised when he saw my test score."

Sally interrupted. "Since there's no school tomorrow, can we go to town and do some Christmas shopping?" she asked, her eyes bright. "I've had some great ideas for gifts lately. Freda isn't here to take us. Don't you want to?'' She took his hand and looked up at him with soulful eyes, filled with pleading. "It'll be fun, Daddy. You'll have a good time, really you will. Can we go?''

If this child did not find a lucrative calling on either stage or screen he would be very much surprised. The look, the tone, the body language—she could give lessons.

Bret stared down at his youngest daughter and sighed. First Freda, then Noelle, now this. He knew when he was beaten. "All right, gang. I'll take you shopping.''

He and Patti used to go to Austin each year. He couldn't face going to the same stores, doing the same things they used to do together. However, there were other places to go, places that didn't hold painful memories.

"Why don't we drive in to San Antonio tomorrow and make a day of it?''

"San Antonio!''

"Really?''

"Oh, boy!''

"Yippee!''

With everybody talking at once he didn't try

to respond except to the little guy who had him by the knees. He glanced down at Travis. "Do you want to go to San Antonio?"

"Uh-huh. Will I get to see Santa?"

"More than likely," Bret replied, remembering when the older children had been young enough to be excited by the thought of seeing Santa Claus.

"Good, 'cause I gotta talk to him," Travis said, sounding very serious.

Bret knelt down beside his youngest. "You do?"

"Uh-huh."

"Do you plan on telling him what you want for Christmas?"

"Uh-huh."

"What *do* you want?"

"I can't tell you. It's a secret."

"But you can tell Santa?"

"Course! How else is he gonna know?"

"Good point."

Noelle came over to them and, as though she'd been doing it for years, brushed a wisp of Bret's hair off his forehead. "You look tired," she said in a soothing voice. "Have you eaten?"

He jerked his head away from her as though she'd burned him with her touch, and straightened from his kneeling position beside Travis. "I'll eat in a few minutes."

She clasped her hands behind her like a small child whose fingers had been slapped, but she didn't drop her gaze. "I'll warm supper for you."

He turned away and started up the stairs. Without looking around he spoke over his shoulder, "Don't bother. I'm sure it's fine the way it is."

Bret reached his room and closed the door before leaning heavily against it. What was wrong with him! She'd merely brushed her fingers against him and he'd felt a charge of electricity shoot all through his body, as though he'd touched a hot-wired fence!

He was acting like a fool—a lovesick fool who'd never been around an attractive woman before.

He'd better eat and get to bed early tonight. He'd need every ounce of energy he could muster tomorrow to deal with the shopping expedition.

After washing up, he returned downstairs. When he walked into the kitchen his place was set, fresh coffee scented the air and Noelle waited to fill a plate for him.

"You didn't have to go to all this trouble for me," he began, politely.

"It was no trouble," she replied, equally polite.

Uncomfortable with the need to apologize, he managed to blurt out, "Look, I didn't mean to be rude earlier. You just startled me, that's all."

She clasped her hands in front of her and gave a brief nod. "I understand. Some people don't like to be touched. It won't happen again."

He sat down and within moments she set a full plate of steaming food in front of him. "It isn't that I mind being touched, exactly...." he said slowly, searching for words.

"It's me, isn't it?"

She'd sat down across from him and watched him with those mesmerizing blue eyes of hers.

He sighed. "You've gotta admit this is an unusual situation."

Her grin was full of mischief. "It certainly is!"

He relaxed a little, now that he realized she wasn't going to take offense. One bite of food told him that as usual, she'd prepared a heavenly meal. He gave up all pretense of conversation and applied his entire attention to the meal in front of him until his plate was clean and he was sipping a fresh cup of coffee.

"There is one thing I'd like to caution you about," he began in a mellow tone, feeling immeasurably better now that he had a full stomach.

Her eyes met his gaze calmly and she waited to hear what he had to say, a personality trait he'd come to recognize in her. She never appeared defensive or unsure of herself. He couldn't remember ever having known anyone who seemed as comfortable with herself as Noelle. Even if he was going to reprimand her—which in this case came close to what he had in mind—she didn't appear anxious or disturbed about what he might say.

"I couldn't help but hear you telling the kids about that train robber earlier. You were making him out to be some kind of hero, eluding the guards and everything.''

''Oh, he was far from a hero. He was a very stubborn individual, determined to ignore any helpful advice about his choice of livelihood.''

He smiled at her prim tone of voice. ''You talk like you knew him.''

''In a manner of speaking.''

''Except that people don't go jumping on Amtrak and attempting to rob the baggage cars.''

Thoughtfully, she nodded. ''That's true.''

''You've got a rich imagination, you know. Have you ever thought about writing some of your tales down? People might enjoy reading about some of these characters you've been talking about. But you'd have to make it plain that they aren't real people. You'd also have to explain how good generally triumphs over evil, no matter how glamorous the bad guys seem to be at times.''

Her smile sparkled and lights seemed to dance in her eyes. ''So you understand that, do you? That's wonderful.''

''What?''

"Nothing, really. I guess I was thinking out loud. If you had let me finish my story, I would have told the children what happened to the bank robber."

"He got caught and ended up in jail?"

She shook her head. "Worse. He didn't get caught and he spent his life running, never being able to trust anyone, never being able to have friends or loved ones, or a family. Never learning how to live." She sighed. "It was a very sad life. Such a waste…especially since it didn't have to turn out that way."

"Was this some movie you once saw?"

She glanced at him in surprise. "Oh, no. I mean, I heard about him from members of my family."

"Oh."

She straightened, and placed her hands on the table. "About tomorrow," she reminded him.

He rolled his eyes. "How could I forget. I've taken advantage of Freda's and Roy's generosity enough. I'm embarrassed that I didn't realize that sooner."

"Don't you ever take the children Christmas shopping?"

"Not if I can help it and I've generally managed to be unavailable each year. Talking to Freda today helped me see how selfish I've been with my time."

"The children were telling me about their visit with her. She sounds like a warm and caring person."

"Yes, she is. She's been a good friend to me through everything."

"I'm glad."

He shifted in his chair. "The truth is, this is always a tough time of year for me. Patti always looked forward to Christmas... decorating the house...planning all sorts of gifts...baking...teaching the children all the time-honored stories. Once she was gone, all the joy left."

"I wonder why? The season is all about experiencing the joy of love and fellowship. She left so much that could remind you of her and her love. The children have shared with me so many wonderful things they remember about their mother. She's very real to them and always will be. She left you a legacy of love, you know. But you have to claim it before you can fully experience it."

He stared at her for an interminable amount of time before he asked, "How old are you?"

She blinked. "What possible difference does that make?"

"Because some of the things you say surprise me, that's all. It's as though you've lived a long life filled with all kinds of experiences and from those experiences you've drawn some fairly profound insights. But you're too young to have experienced very much."

"I don't think of age very much. I suppose I consider it more of an attitude rather than a fixed number."

"An attitude, huh? Then I feel about eighty years old today, too old for all this exuberance and enthusiasm." He rubbed the back of his neck. "But I want my kids to be happy and I'll do whatever I can to help make this a fun time for them."

"You're a very loving father, Bret. You've done a great job with your children."

He could actually feel his ears burning with embarrassment. "I make all kinds of mistakes with them every day."

"So? Don't you think they need to see that

fathers don't have to be perfect? You also show them that each of them is very important to you. You aren't afraid to show your love for them. You're also willing to admit your mistakes when you make them. How can they not find you endearing?''

''They need more than I can give them, though. They need their mother.''

''I believe they've come to terms with her loss better than you have, Bret. They're getting on with their lives while you're still looking back, wishing for what was rather than accepting what is.''

''Maybe so. Maybe I don't know *how* to get on with my life.''

''That's because you haven't tried. You need to get out more. You need to socialize, find some nice woman to date, enjoy being—''

''There! You're doing it again!''

She looked startled. ''Doing what?''

''Talking like you're some old woman. I don't—''

''Dad?''

Bret glanced up at Chris who'd just come in the back door.

"Yes, son?"

"Roy was just telling me that he's planning to go shopping tomorrow, too. Would it be all right with you if the girls and I went with him? He said he'd take us to San Antonio and we could meet you all there later."

Bret smiled at his oldest son. "Are you saying that you don't want to see Santa this year, Chris?"

Chris laughed. "Well, it won't break my heart if I miss standing in line for hours like we had to do last year. Besides, Roy lets us shop on our own so our gifts are a surprise to everybody."

"And you think I'll insist on tagging along behind you, is that it?"

Chris looked startled, then concerned. He walked over to the table and stopped beside his dad. "I guess I wasn't thinking, was I? Does it sound like we don't want you to go? It isn't that at all! It's just that we've kinda set up a routine with Roy, that's all. But, hey. It's no problem. I think it's great you've volunteered to take us. We can all go in together and make a day of it. It will be just like old—'' He paused, then swallowed and looked away.

''I like your idea just fine, son. You and the girls go with Roy. Noelle and I will take Travis with us and we'll meet you at a designated place and time.''

Chris's eyes met Bret's. ''You sure you don't mind?''

''I'm positive.'' He didn't drop his gaze.

Chris gave a sigh of relief. ''That's great, Dad. I know we'll have a good time tomorrow. Having you there will make it even more special.''

The room seemed to fill with silence after Chris went upstairs. Bret wasn't sure what to do or say. Noelle quietly gathered his dishes and washed them, then began putting them away.

''I hadn't realized how protective the children have been of my feelings,'' Bret finally said.

''They love you very much,'' Noelle replied, standing on tiptoe to put one of the serving bowls away, her back to him.

''It's bad enough that they had to lose their

mother without worrying about the remaining parent, as well. That's a lot to push off on a child.''

''Children are strong. Otherwise they'd never survive.''

Bret slid down into his chair, his legs stretched out in front of him. ''Patti used to say that every child was born with at least one guardian angel making certain they would be safe.''

''You don't believe that?''

He gave her a wistful smile. ''Wouldn't it be a great world if that were true? Babies wouldn't be born addicted to whatever their mothers' choice of drug was…they wouldn't be born with physical defects…they wouldn't be born in parts of the world where they'll probably starve to death before they reach school age.''

''You think that guardian angels could prevent all of that?''

He raised his brows. ''Don't you?''

''Not all angels are capable of performing those kinds of miracles. I like to think that the angels guard those little babies as much as they are able, comforting them, helping them to feel safe and loved, preparing them for a better place, regardless of what eventually happens to them.''

"I'd like to believe that, too," Bret admitted. "I can scarcely remember those first months after Patti died, but somehow Travis managed to survive anyway. I must have cared for him and loved him, but I don't remember much of it. It's almost like I was in some kind of fog, or a bad dream.''

"It's time to wake up, Bret.''

He glanced up and saw that she was standing beside him. He gave her a lopsided smile and obeying an impulse, snaked his arm around her and pulled her down on his lap. She would have slid down the length of his legs if he hadn't caught her with his other arm. Before he could quite believe what he'd done, Bret discovered he had one arm wrapped around Noelle's hips, the other around her waist, and she was lying along his chest and shoulder.

Slowly he straightened in the chair, keeping a firm grasp on the woman in his arms. She felt good there. Very good. For the first time in a long, long time, he felt alive.

"I'm awake, Noelle," he murmured, his voice rumbling deep in his chest.

He could see that he had caught her totally unprepared, which pleased him considerably. She seemed to know so damned much about so many things, but there was one area where she didn't know diddly…and he was just about to show her!

"Uh, Bret, I don't think—" she began, pushing herself away from him slightly.

He wasn't having any part of her retreat. She was now resting squarely on his thighs, which freed up one of his arms. He tilted her chin up with his thumb.

She smelled tantalizingly feminine and his body no longer felt eighty years old. He tilted his head slightly and kissed her.

He'd been right. She didn't know a blamed thing about kissing, but that was fine. He had plenty of time and he was a very patient instructor.

Her mouth felt so soft. He watched her eyelids flutter, then close. When she gave a tiny sigh he used the opportunity to touch his tongue to her lips, edging her mouth gradually open until he could explore more fully. He increased the pressure, enjoying the pleasure of holding her close, feeling her respond to him. He allowed his hand to slide along her neck and throat downward until it came to rest cupping her breast.

Yes! She felt just the way he had dreamed she would, her breast filling his palm as though made with him in mind. He could feel her heart beating so rapidly her chest shook.

She was so innocent and he was taking advantage of her.

That thought washed over him like a sudden cold and drenching rain. Reluctantly he forced himself to move his hand until it safely circled her waist once more. He even tried to end the kiss, but even his strong willpower couldn't overcome the intensity of their shared experience.

When he finally released her, he buried his face in her hair and shuddered with the depth of his overwhelming desire for her.

She clung to him and he was thankful that

he hadn't frightened her with his strong reaction to the kiss. He was a grown man and he should have known better. But he was also human, and no one short of a saint could have withstood the temptation that Noelle presented to him.

As soon as she stirred, he released the pressure of his arms around her. She pulled away until she could look into his face. "I didn't know," she said with wonder.

"You didn't know what?"

"How it felt. I had no idea what happens…I mean the way we react to each other." Her eyes were wide. "Kisses are pretty potent stuff, aren't they?"

He grinned. Did she have any idea how adorable she looked perched on his lap, her hair all mussed, discussing the ramifications of their first kiss?

"They can be, yes," he replied, still grinning.

"I had no idea."

"Are you telling me you've never been kissed?"

"Not like that," she replied emphatically.

"Are you beginning to understand why I was concerned about your staying here?"

She looked at him warily. "Why? Do you intend to do that again?"

He laughed. He couldn't help it. She looked like one of the tiny kittens whose fur had just been rubbed the wrong way.

"Not if you don't want me to, of course. I'd never force myself on you. But I got a distinct impression that you didn't mind that kiss at all, and that you wouldn't argue if I proposed another one."

She thought about that for a moment, then smiled, obviously delighted with her conclusion. "You're right. I didn't mind it at all and I'd very much like to enjoy another one." Without waiting to see his response she closed her eyes, wrapped her arms around his neck and kissed him with a burst of innocent enthusiasm.

Chapter Four

"Why didn't somebody tell me what it's like? I had no idea, no warning, nothing to prepare me. I—"

"Noelle—"

"By the way, how old am I?"

"You're ageless. Noelle—"

"That's what I thought. I mean, if I'd ever bothered to give it a thought. But all of a sudden I'm thinking about such things—earthly things—a great deal. Like, how old I am, and how I look, and if Bret finds me attractive—he certainly kisses me like he finds me attractive—and I find him very attractive. I can't believe how attractive. I mean, the most subtle things about him start my heart racing as though I've been running for hours. Take his hair, for instance. I find myself spending hours of my day while I'm cleaning house or washing clothes or preparing meals, wondering exactly how you'd describe his hair. It's so thick and it's all these different colors, like taffy and wheat and cinnamon and straw. Straw. I never would have thought that straw was a beautiful color but oh, on Bret it looks wonderful, really amazingly so.

"And his eyes. I can't stop gazing into his eyes. At first I thought they were brown. Well, maybe a light brown. Then I realized they were the same exact, identical color of well-aged whiskey—almost like topaz, but with swirling depths in them. They even change color according to his mood. When he's tired they're golden and when he's angry they get darker, almost like they're flashing sparks. Sometimes, when he looks at me a certain way, they go all liquid and molten. That look makes me go weak in my knees. It really does.

I've heard the expression many times but I've never experienced the feeling before. I'm telling you right now, it's the weirdest feeling I've had in a long time. Let's face it, I've just gotten used to having knees and now they're already acting up on me.

"The thing is, I don't know what to do. Well, of course I know what I'm supposed to be doing. My assignment was all very clear and concise. And it isn't as though I haven't always loved Bret because I have. But this is different. I mean, really different. And it's confusing me. I've been daydreaming around the house, rerunning the dreams he has about me every night, trying to imagine what it would feel like if he really were doing those things to me. I'm telling you here and now being human isn't anything like I thought it was at all."

"What did you think it was like?"

"Going around making really stupid mistakes, needing somebody to guide you through them. Well, from my new perspective, they don't look so stupid, and most of all they don't look like mistakes."

"Would you care to give me an example?"

She thought for a moment. "Well, the other day Travis told me that he wished that I would stay with them all year-round instead of just during the Christmas season. He said that he wished I could be his mommy."

"Not a very surprising wish for a young child who has never had a mother."

"I know. Before I took on human form, I would have quickly explained how that wasn't possible, how it was only through a special dispensation that I had been allowed to materialize for him at all."

"You didn't tell him that?"

She hung her head. "No."

"What did you tell him?"

She lifted her chin and stared at her supervisor. "I told him I wished I could be his mommy, too."

Noelle waited for an explosion at the very least. She had done some unangelic things before, she'd managed to get into some pretty tumultuous situations before, but never had she made such an out and out earthly remark.

She waited for a response. She waited for

what seemed forever. For that matter, it could have been forever since there was no measurement of time in this dimension. So she wasn't certain if a few minutes or an eternity passed before her supervisor responded.

"I see."

Those two words seemed to circle her as though they had taken on their own form, becoming special entities capable of independent action.

What had she expected...a reprimand? Some form of judgment? Chastisement? Maybe she'd been on earth too long. She was already beginning to react like a human being, waiting for a lightning bolt to strike her.

"The thing is, I don't know what to do. I'm really confused."

"Are you looking for guidance?"

"Oh, yes! That's exactly what I want."

"You need only to ask, surely you haven't forgotten?"

"I know that I've made a positive change in the children's lives. In addition, Freda is getting a much needed rest and an opportunity to review what she's doing with her life and whether she wishes to continue her present path.

"As for Bret...well, I think he's beginning to see how he'd cut himself off from the world these past three years. How he'd retreated into himself, giving only what was demanded of him.

"Now he's beginning to feel again, to notice the world around him. He's, uh, well, he's realizing certain things are lacking in his life—like female companionship and physical closeness. He's discovered that he's in the prime of his life and that he could have so much more if he decided to reach out for what he wants."

"Then you are doing your job well, I would say."

"Except that he wants to reach out to me."

"For physical closeness and female companionship?"

"Exactly."

"Surely you can arrange for him to meet some eligible women before you leave, women with whom he would have something in common, perhaps a woman who's been unable to have a family of her own and would feel

blessed to find a ready-made one waiting for her.''

"I suppose so."

"Do I detect a certain lack of enthusiasm in your tone?''

"Yes. That's exactly why I'm so confused. I know what needs to be done. I know I'm capable of bringing about the situations needed for him to have a varied selection from which to choose. The problem is, I don't want him to fall in love with someone else."

There. She had finally put her feelings into words.

''You prefer to see him the way he was before you came into his life?''

"Not at all. It's just that I want to be the one with whom he falls in love."

"Given your present circumstances, I can understand why you might feel that way. It's perfectly natural and normal for a human being to have such yearnings. Once Christmas arrives and you return to your original form those strange human yearnings will no longer be with you. You will be able to regain your objectivity in the matter.''

"Are you certain of that?"

Her supervisor smiled. *"Have I ever lied to you?"*

"Of course not. Please forgive my doubts."

"There's nothing to forgive, of course. I can see tremendous growth in you since you embarked on this latest assignment. You're doing splendidly."

"It feels more like I've gone backward. I used to have such a clear vision of what I was supposed to be doing in relation to everyone around me. Now, I don't have a clue of where I am."

"I believe we do our greatest growing during that period when we seem not to know anything. Perhaps that is our greatest lesson— to understand how very little we know. What is important is that we do what needs to be done in a timely fashion. I would say that you are on schedule, wouldn't you?"

"Christmas is only a week away. I have seven days."

"An eternity to some."

"Thank you for listening to me."

"I am always here for you, just as my coun-

selor is always here for me, and so forth and so on. No one has to be alone unless he or she so chooses.''

''Bret doesn't understand how alone he's been, how he hasn't bothered to ask for help or guidance. He would laugh at the idea of being alone while raising four children, not to mention having Freda and Roy around most of the time. As far as that goes, Bret doesn't believe in angels, which is amusing when you think about it.''

''Whether you recognize it or not, you are making great changes in this man's life. He will never again be quite the same man he was before you appeared before him.''

''That works both ways. I'll never forget Bret, either. Never.''

Chapter Five

Roy tapped on the kitchen door while the family was eating breakfast the next morning. Noelle quickly opened the door since she had just stepped to the counter nearby for the coffeepot. "Good morning, Roy," she said, smiling at the tall, thin cowboy. "Would you like some coffee?"

Stepping inside, Roy raked his hat off his head with his hand, and nodded shyly. "Sounds good, ma'am."

"Chris tells me you still plan to go Christmas shopping today," Bret said, eyeing Roy with a half smile on his face. "You're a real glutton for punishment, aren't you."

"Well, I kinda like taking the kids every year. It's become sort of a tradition with me. They're my family, you know. We've got a regular thing going."

"Since I promised Travis I would take him to see Santa this year, why don't you take Chris and the girls in the Bronco and Noelle, Travis and I'll go in the truck." He named one of the newer malls in San Antonio and said, "We'll plan on meeting at Santa's Village about four o'clock. Will that give everybody enough time to see everything they want to see?"

A chorus of affirmatives almost deafened him. He could see the excitement building as the children all exchanged glances.

Noelle looked at Travis. "Is that all right with you? If you stay with your Dad and me?"

He nodded vigorously. "Yep."

Bret ruffled his youngest son's hair. "This will be a new experience for us, won't it, young'un? We've never gone shopping together for Christmas."

Travis's smile was cherubic. "It's because Noelle's coming, too."

Bret glanced over at Noelle and saw her cheeks flaming. Slowly Bret acknowledged, "You're probably right. Guess Noelle's caused a lot of changes since she arrived, hasn't she?"

"Uh-huh. I think we should keep her."

With a speculative glance at her flushed cheeks Bret replied, "You think so?" When he caught her eye, he winked.

Obviously flustered, Noelle gathered up the dishes on the table and carried them to the sink.

The room soon emptied of the children, who'd gone upstairs to finish dressing. Bret shook his head and said, "I don't know how four children manage to sound like a hundred-voice chorus. It's kind of nice to have a few minutes of peace."

Absently he watched Noelle move around the room until everything had been washed and put away. His gaze followed her as she went into Freda's room and closed the door.

Roy lowered his voice. "Have you noticed something strange about Noelle?"

"Strange?"

"Yeah. Well, different maybe."

"Not particularly. Have you?"

"Well, for one thing, she never seems to get tired. She's on the go every time I see her, and she's always in a good mood. Now I never knowed a woman to be in a good mood *all* the time. By and large, I find women to be kinda moody. It's a little distracting to me to see somebody so blamed cheerful all the time. It kinda makes me wonder what she's up to."

Bret carefully hid his smile. "Do you have any ideas on the subject?"

"Well, I've been wondering if she's trying to take over Freda's job."

Bret lifted his cup and took a swallow of coffee, trying to gain some time to think of what to say.

Roy went on. "Have you asked her how long she intends to stay?"

"Not in so many words. She said she'd come to help out while Freda was in the hospital, that's all."

"Have you noticed how she's managed to wrap those kids of yours around her little finger? Why, they about fall all over themselves being helpful and respectful.''

''Let me get this straight, Roy. Are you saying that this woman has aroused your suspicions by being too good?''

Roy thought about that for a minute. ''You gotta admit it ain't real natural.''

''Do you think she has an ulterior motive? Other than possibly taking Freda's job, of course.''

''That'd be bad enough.''

''You're missing Freda, I take it.''

Roy's ears glowed red. ''Well, I guess I've gotten used to her ways. A fella doesn't like change in his life, you know? I prefer a set routine, something I can count on.''

''Do you think Noelle's undependable? Untrustworthy? What?''

Roy scratched his ear and frowned, thinking. ''I just don't want to see you and the children hurt, that's all.''

''It may be my imagination, but the kids have seemed much happier since she arrived.''

Roy leaned on the table and looked at Bret from beneath his bushy brows. ''They ain't the only ones. I actually heard *you* laugh the other day.''

''You didn't! Why, Roy, I'm shocked.''

''You gotta admit that it takes some gittin' used to.''

Bret's smile slowly faded. ''You're right, Roy. I guess I hadn't noticed the number of changes that have occurred recently. I haven't been one to laugh very much these past few years.''

''Don't suppose you found much to laugh about.''

''That's true.''

Roy nodded, still thinking through the subject very carefully. ''So maybe, in that respect, having Miss Noelle come to stay a spell's been good for you.''

''You think so?''

After a long moment, Roy said, ''I reckon I do. I guess not every change is necessarily bad.''

''There's a positive thought, Roy. Very positive. I'll keep it in mind.'' He pushed back his chair. ''Guess we'd better get ready for this big shopping trip.''

"That's one of the things I've been talking about. You always found fifteen good reasons why you was always too busy to go into town during Christmas season. Now you seem almost eager."

Bret sighed and lightly tapped Roy on the shoulder with his fist. "I can't begin to explain it, myself. It must be the Christmas season…maybe it's contagious and I've just now caught it."

Bret left the room and headed up the stairs, thinking about their conversation. He met the three older children clattering down the steps, and got hugs from his daughters and a casual wave from his oldest son. He glanced into Travis's room on his way past, and abruptly halted. Travis was sitting on the side of his bed, holding the framed picture of Patti.

"Something wrong?" he asked casually, leaning against the doorjamb.

Travis looked up. "No. I was just talkin' to Mommy. 'Splaining stuff to her."

"I see."

"Are we ready to go?"

"Just about. You're looking pretty sharp

there, fella. Did you get dressed on your own?''

''Mostly. Sally helped me with my boots 'cause sometimes I get 'em on the wrong feet.''

''You did a fine job.''

''I wanted to look good for Santa.''

''He's bound to be impressed.'' He turned away. ''I'll see you downstairs.'' Bret went into his room, wondering what exactly Travis had needed to '''splain'' to Patti.

He also wondered how he was going to get through today without revealing how hard it was to become a part of the Christmas scene. He was doing everything he could to release the past without letting those around him know how difficult it was for him.

Roy was right. Noelle had made it much easier for him. She had a way of looking at him as though she could see deep down into his soul…to the place where his most private feelings were stored. How could someone who appeared so young and naive continue to project so much warmth, empathy and caring? At times it was all he could do not to gather her in his arms and just hold her close, knowing how good he'd feel.

The problem with taking Noelle in his arms and holding her as he'd done last night was the fact that he forgot all about her empathy and caring and was immediately made aware of her womanly warmth and how blasted good she felt in his embrace.

He didn't want to take advantage of their situation but after last night he knew the temptations were steadily mounting.

By the time Bret returned downstairs Roy and the older children had already left. Noelle and Travis waited patiently for him in the kitchen.

"Sorry to take so long," Bret said sheepishly.

Travis took his hand. "It's okay, Daddy. Don't be scared in the big stores. I'll hold your hand so you don't get losted."

"I appreciate that, son."

Travis beamed up at him. "'Course it helps to have an angel along, you know."

Bret raised his brow slightly. "Good point. I'm obviously in good hands today." He reached down and picked up Travis. "Let's hit the road, pardner." He paused in the doorway and held the door open for Noelle. She looked up at him and smiled. His heart lunged in his chest like a spooked mustang and raced at an alarming rate.

Over a simple smile?

He gave his head a sharp shake, reminding himself that he wasn't some adolescent kid with a schoolboy crush. Now he had to convince his body of the fact.

Bret hadn't been to San Antonio in several months. For that matter, he hadn't been anywhere other than the ranch and the small town nearby where he bought supplies. Forcing himself out today made him realize how limited he'd been.

When they came in on the northern outskirts of the city, the traffic had picked up considerably, a strong reminder of why he avoided big cities during the holiday season. He reminded himself that there was no hurry, they had most of the day, and eventually edged into the lane he needed to exit for the mall.

The mall had been designed to cater to large crowds so the parking lot was immense. However, they circled for almost twenty minutes before he happened to spot the flash of backup lights of a vehicle just ahead. With a muttered comment, he waited until the elderly couple pulled out, then whipped into the available space.

"Wow! I didn't ever think we'd find a place, did you, Daddy?"

"I was beginning to wonder, myself." He glanced at Noelle—who had kept Travis entertained during the two-hour drive from the ranch—and smiled.

Once again her response made his heart kick into overdrive.

As soon as they reached the mall itself the piped music echoed all around them. Bret almost groaned aloud. Travis skipped along between them, holding each of their hands. His eyes were shining as he took in all the tinseled splendor.

"When are we going to see Santa?"

Bret gave Noelle a knowing look. "I have a hunch we'd better put that first on our list."

They had no trouble finding Santa. All they had to watch for was the long line of small children eager to talk and have their pictures taken with the man.

"Poor dear," Bret heard Noelle mutter.

"Who?"

She glanced down at Travis who was hopping from one foot to the other, chattering with a little girl in line behind them. She nodded to the man in the Santa suit. "He's really not enjoying the job. What a shame that he chose to take it."

Bret looked around the large rotunda at the crowd of people. "Who could enjoy something like this?"

She looked surprised. "To be able to speak to each child, to hear their fondest hopes and dreams? I would imagine that many people would." She looked away. "I know I enjoy it very much."

"But you've only had to listen to the four at home."

She chuckled. "That's true."

"Besides. How do you know he isn't enjoying himself? He's handling the children very professionally, I would say."

"He's very good. His heart's just not in it."

"And you can tell that from here, of course."

She nodded. "Just as I can tell that your heart isn't in this shopping expedition. Tell me, why did you agree to come?"

He looked down into her mesmerizing eyes for a long time before he murmured, "I'm not sure. It felt like the right thing to do at the time."

"I'm glad you did. Perhaps it will change your attitude about Christmas."

"What, exactly, is my attitude?"

She looked surprised. "You just want to get it over with as quickly and painlessly as possible."

"Do you do mind reading acts in addition to looking after households?"

"Bret, I don't know exactly how to break this to you, but even your three-year-old son knows how you feel about Christmas."

"That obvious, huh?"

"That obvious."

"And here I've been patting myself on the back all the way to San Antonio, congratulating myself on how well I've hidden my feelings.''

Her spontaneous cascade of laughter caught him off guard. She rocked with hilarity, leaving him bemused. In the first place, he didn't particularly appreciate being the object of her amusement, but more startling to him was the sound of her musical laughter. The people in line were glancing at her and smiling at her unrestrained enjoyment of the moment.

Sheepishly Bret chuckled, finally seeing the absurdity in the situation, which set her off again. He began to laugh in earnest, for no reason other than it felt good. He'd long since forgotten the last time he'd found something to laugh about. The shocked look on his son's face was a silent reminder that in all likelihood Bret hadn't laughed with wholesome enjoyment since Travis was born.

''What's so funny, Daddy?''

Noelle did a commendable job of regaining control. Only her eyes still danced with laughter.

''We were just being silly,'' he replied, still grinning.

"I didn't know that daddies could be silly, just like kids."

Bret's gaze met Noelle's. "I guess I kinda forgot that myself, son."

When it became Travis's turn to talk with Santa he gave Noelle a brief, panicked look. She immediately knelt beside him and whispered into his ear. He nodded and his features relaxed. She gave him a quick hug and he turned away from her, walking over to Santa with quiet dignity.

Bret couldn't hear what he was saying, but he could certainly see his son's earnestness.

"Do you know what it is he wants for Christmas?" Bret asked.

"Yes."

When she didn't say anything more, Bret verbally nudged her by saying, "Aren't you going to tell me?"

"No." Her smile took any sting out of the quiet response.

"It's going to be tough for me to see that he gets it if I don't know what he wants."

"I'm sure he'll tell you in his own good time."

"I don't think so. He wouldn't tell me the last time we discussed it."

"Perhaps he didn't find the timing to be the best."

"Are you telling me that a three-year-old has the knowledge and intelligence to plan strategy?"

"It's an instinctive form of survival. He's watched how his older brother and sisters manage to get what they want from you. They know when to leave you alone—when you're tired and hungry or upset about something. They also know when to approach you...when you're well fed and in an expansive mood."

"I had no idea I was so easy to read."

"Your children know that you are all they have, therefore you've assumed a position of major importance in their existence. They instinctively know that it is mandatory for them to understand you well."

Travis came bounding over to them and said, "When do we eat?"

Noelle laughed. "I can see you have your priorities straight."

It was over a sandwich in the food court

section of the mall that Bret said to Travis, "Tell us about your visit with Santa."

Travis swallowed, then took a sip from his straw before he said, "I liked him, even though he wasn't the real Santa."

Bret eyed him warily. "He wasn't?"

Travis looked at his dad in disgust. "'Course not. The real Santa doesn't have time to sit around and talk to people this close to Christmas. But he told me that he'd be sure to pass my message on to the real Santa."

Bret refused to meet Noelle's eyes. "That's comforting to know." After a few more minutes of silence while they finished their meals, he asked, "So what was your message?"

This time Travis wouldn't meet his father's eyes. "I can't tell. It's a secret." He looked at Bret with a wide-eyed gaze. "But I think you'll like it, Daddy."

Bret sat back. "Me? I thought we were talking about what *you* want for Christmas?"

Travis looked like a mischievous cherub. "It's for both of us…all of us…the whole family!"

Now Bret did look at Noelle but her attention seemed to be fully caught by something beyond their table. Whatever was going on, he'd need to get some answers soon.

By the time they met Roy and the other children Bret felt as though he'd been pulled through a knothole backward. Where did everyone get their energy? The noise and the crowd had given him a headache. He was too used to the solitude of wide open spaces to ever get used to the turmoil swirling around him.

Roy spoke up. "I've been thinkin', boss. Why don't you let me take Travis and the kids back with me. We'll stop and eat on the way home and maybe drop by to see Freda for a while. That'll give you and Noelle some time to yourselves."

Bret was surprised at the suggestion. He was more surprised at the eager expressions worn by all his children. They must really miss Freda.

"I suppose so, Roy." He glanced down at Noelle. "What do you say?"

"Whatever we do is fine with me. I'm along for the ride."

And so it was that Bret found himself having dinner with Noelle some time later at a restaurant overlooking the river in downtown San Antonio, a restaurant Roy had suggested.

"What a beautiful view," she was saying, staring out the window.

"Have you ever visited San Antonio before?"

She shook her head, smiling.

"So what do you think of the city?"

Her eyes sparkled. "I'm fascinated by everything. This is such an exciting time of the year."

"How do you generally spend your Christmases? Do you go home?"

After a brief hesitation, she nodded. "Yes…at home."

He smiled. "Well, you've made our Christmas season much more joyous this year. I'm not certain what we would have done without you."

"I feel very blessed. The time seems to have rushed by. There's only a few more days until Christmas."

"We haven't talked about that, have we…I

mean, how long you've been here, and your salary—''

''Oh, please!'' Noelle looked quite distressed. ''I can't accept money for helping you. I have all that I need. Perhaps Freda—''

He took her hand. ''I've already reassured Freda that all her bills are taken care of. She knows how much I value her. She will never do without anything as long as I'm able to look after her.''

Her smile trembled with sweetness. ''I'm so glad.''

''You are?''

She blinked. ''Yes, of course. I'm touched to know she means so much to you. You're a very honorable man.''

It was his turn to sit back in surprise. ''Me? What have I done?''

''Still care about those around you, despite the pain you've been experiencing.''

He looked at her for a long while without saying anything. When he did, his voice sounded gruff to his ears. ''Speaking of being honorable, I need to apologize to you.''

''For what?''

"For my behavior last night. I shouldn't have grabbed you the way I did...and I sure shouldn't have kissed you." He fought not to squirm like a schoolboy confessing to the authorities. "I had no business taking advantage of you. You're a guest in my home and deserve my respect." When he finally forced himself to look up from the coffee sitting in front of him all he saw in her face was curiosity. "What's wrong?"

"I'm afraid I don't understand. By kissing me you showed me disrespect?"

He couldn't think of how to respond. She looked honestly curious, rather than offended or disapproving. Didn't she understand anything about men? His thoughts unerringly raced back to the kiss...to the second kiss that she had initiated. A ripple of awareness ran over him. She might have seemed inexperienced during their first kiss but as for the second one...whatever she might have lacked in experience she certainly made up for in enthusiasm.

He shook the disturbing memories away. "What I'm trying to do is to reassure you that it won't happen again. I promise."

Darned if she didn't look disappointed! This conversation wasn't going the way he'd expected. He didn't know what to say.

She didn't help matters any. She reached across the table and touched the back of his hand with her fingertips. "I enjoyed kissing you, Bret Bishop. Please don't apologize. If you prefer not to kiss me again, I can accept that, but you did nothing wrong."

His hand tingled where she touched him and he was having trouble getting his tongue to come unglued from the top of his mouth when he heard his name being called in a light, feminine voice.

"Bret? Bret Bishop! Is it you?"

He glanced around, then stood with a grin. "Gina Sweeney! I don't believe it." He held out his hand. "I haven't seen you in a coon's age. How are you?"

She took his proffered hand in both of hers and said, "It's Montgomery, now, although I've been divorced from Hal for almost four years." Gina's face shone with pleasure. "My, but it's good to see you after all this time. When I looked across the room I couldn't believe my eyes."

Bret turned and said, "Noelle, I want you to meet Gina. We went all the way through school together, from the first grade until we graduated from high school." He shook his head in wonder. "I haven't seen you since graduation, which has been—"

She laughingly interrupted. "More years than I want to admit to." She offered her hand to Noelle. "I'm very pleased to meet you. Noelle. Such an unusual name, but it seems perfect for you, somehow."

Bret looked to the table where Gina had been and saw another couple. Before he could ask, she explained, "I'm visiting friends here in San Antonio. They've been after me to come see them for so long. I haven't been back to Texas in years. Finally I decided on the spur-of-the-moment to fly down and visit for a few days."

He motioned to a chair. "Well, sit down for a minute. Let me find out what you've been doing."

Gracefully she slid into the chair he offered. "I've been working in the court system in a county just north of Nashville for several

years. Hal's an attorney there. We had an am-
icable divorce, which made it so much more
comfortable to stay on there. I really love my
work.''

''Do you have any children?''

''One…a girl.'' She looked at the two of
them and asked, ''Do you and Noelle have
children?''

''Oh, we—'' Noelle began to say when Bret
cut in.

''We have four—two of each.''

''Still ranching?''

''Of course. That's all the Bishops know
how to do.''

She shook her head. ''Better you than me.
I could hardly wait to get out of ranching
country.'' She grinned. ''Give me city lights
any day.''

After a few minutes of discussing old class-
mates and their possible whereabouts, Gina
said, ''Well, it's been wonderful running into
you like this. If you ever get to Tennessee be
sure to contact me.''

Since she'd already given him her address
and phone number, he nodded. As soon as she

left their table Bret looked at Noelle and smiled. "Are you ready to go?"

"Whenever you are." She stood and he helped her with her jacket. After paying the waiter, Bret took her hand and led her out of the restaurant into the cool night.

Once outside they walked to the truck in silence. Noelle waited until they left the city limits before she spoke.

"Bret?"

"Hmm?"

"Why did you let your friend think that you and I were married?"

He was quiet for a moment, thinking. "I don't know, really. I guess because I didn't think it really mattered to the conversation."

"But she's single."

"Yeah, so she said."

"And you're single."

"So?"

"Haven't you given any thought to the possibility that you might marry again someday?"

Another long silence ensued. "Now that you mention it," he drawled, "maybe the thought has crossed my mind once or twice recently, why?"

"Well, Gina was obviously happy to see you and I thought—"

When her voice dwindled to nothing, he prompted, "You thought—?"

She heard amusement in his voice. "Well, it just seems to me that maybe you'd want to follow up on your friendship."

"Tell me something, Miss Noelle, are you trying to play matchmaker for me?"

"Oh! Well, no. Not exactly."

"I'm glad to hear it. You know, I'd much prefer to decide for myself who I'd like to spend my time with."

"Of course."

He glanced at her from the corner of his eye. The glow from the dash offered enough light for him to see her heightened color. "How about you? Have you ever given any thought to getting married?"

"Me?" She sounded shocked. "Of course not! What I mean is, I—uh—well, have my career to think about and—" She coughed and gave up.

"Your career. I see. I certainly hope your helping us here hasn't delayed any of your plans."

"Oh, no," she quickly replied. "My career is all about helping people wherever I can, so this was all part of— What I mean is, I was just glad to be able to help you," she finished lamely.

"You know, I realize that I haven't had much time to visit with you since you arrived. Why don't you tell me more about yourself."

"All right."

When she didn't say anything more he waited, and waited, and finally started laughing.

"Did I say something funny?"

"Not at all. What was funny was that you didn't say anything. Most people who agree to talk about themselves don't sit in silence."

"Oh! I'm sorry. I was waiting to find out what you wanted to know about me."

"Have you always lived in California?"

"No."

"Do you visit Ida often?"

"No."

"Come on, Noelle. I need a little help here."

"I guess I don't know what it is you're interested in learning about me. I feel as though you know the truly important things about me. I enjoy children. I love to cook. Living in the country is the closest thing to heaven I know...."

"Then you really are content at the ranch."

She turned and looked at him, her face glowing. "Oh, yes, more than I can possibly say."

Something deep inside him seemed to splinter, shift and break loose. Freda was right. His emotions were definitely coming out of the deep freeze...they were melting like ice in a spring thaw.

He reached over, took her hand and carefully placed it on his thigh, then rested his hand on top.

They rode that way in silence for the rest of the way home.

Chapter Six

By the time they reached the ranch the house was dark except for a muted glow coming from the living room. Bret parked the truck in the large shed beside the barn, then went around and helped Noelle down from the big vehicle.

Instead of going toward the back door, however, he led her along the driveway until they reached the front of the house where he paused. From there they could see through the living-room window into the warmth of the room beyond.

''The tree looks so festive all lit up like that, doesn't it?'' he murmured. ''I've never really taken the time to look at it before tonight.''

She stood beside him and saw the love and attention that draped and surrounded the tree, each and every ornament carefully chosen over the years by a family's tradition. ''It's lovely.''

He gave her hand a gentle squeeze, then led her up the steps to the front door, which was seldom used. They found Roy asleep on the sofa, the television flickering its late-night movie. The quiet closing of the door alerted Roy to their arrival and he sat up and yawned. ''Did ya have a good time?''

''Yes,'' Noelle answered softly. ''You were right. The view of the river was well worth seeing.'' She glanced up at Bret. ''Thank you for taking me.''

Roy coughed. ''Well, guess I'd better get home.''

''How was Freda?''

''Oh, she's looking good...seemed tickled to see us. Said she'd missed all the ruckus of getting ready for the holidays and all.''

"Has the doctor told her when she could leave the hospital?"

"Well, he said it would definitely be in time for Christmas, providing she doesn't try to get around on that leg anytime soon. He's insisting she take it easy and get plenty of rest. Guess her sister intends to make sure she does." Roy looked at Noelle. "You planning to be here through the holidays?"

"Well, I'll be able to stay until—"

Bret interrupted, saying, "We haven't had a chance to discuss it, Roy."

Roy got the message. "Well, I'll see you in the mornin'," he said, picking up his hat and settling it on his head.

Bret followed him to the door and locked up after him. He returned to the living room, where Noelle stood gazing at the tree, a wistful smile on her face.

"Noelle?"

She turned and looked at him.

As though drawn by a magnet, Bret moved closer until he was close enough to touch her. He brushed her cheek with the back of his hand. Her skin was so smooth, smoother than anything else he could name. Her complexion was so fair—like ivory—with just a hint of color tinting her cheekbones. However, it was her eyes—deep blue surrounded by a fringe of thick lashes—that tugged a deep response from somewhere inside of him.

He forgot what he had intended to say. Instead, he murmured, "Travis is right."

"About what?"

"You really do look like the Christmas angel. They must have modeled her after you."

She smiled, but didn't say anything.

Carefully, as though she were made of porcelain and could easily break, he slipped his arms around her waist. "I know what I said earlier, and I hate to break a promise, but I don't think I'm strong enough to leave this room without kissing you."

She went up on tiptoe and placed her hands trustingly against his chest. "I'd like that... very much."

A strong surge of protectiveness swept over him even while he took what she offered without hesitation. She felt so natural there, as though she'd found her home in his arms.

He brushed his lips against hers, wanting to savor each sensation, wanting to relish the moment. He could feel her quivering, causing him to stroke her spine in a soothing gesture of comfort. Then he lost all sense of thought or awareness of anything other than their blending.

Eventually he scooped her up in his arms and settled down on the sofa with her draped across his lap. He took his time exploring each tiny new discovery about her…her delicate waist, the gentle curve of her hips. Meanwhile he continued to press kisses on her face and neck and down to the opening of her blouse.

Her fluttering fingers touched his face, danced through his hair, shyly caressed his chest until he thought he might explode with desire for her.

Bret forced himself to lift his head away from her. He drew several deep breaths, still holding her close to him, before he allowed his head to lean against the sofa's backrest.

When he opened his eyes and looked at her she was watching him with a solemn scrutiny he found captivating.

"You don't enjoy kissing me?"

He couldn't hide his smile. "On the contrary. I enjoy it very much."

"Then why do you feel guilty for doing something you enjoy?"

Her discernment never ceased to amaze him. "I don't want to take advantage of you."

"You've done nothing that I haven't allowed."

He sighed. "I know this will sound crazy, but I feel as though I'm cheating on Patti."

"I can understand that. You've treated Patti's absence in your life as temporary. Somewhere you've harbored the feeling that she will be back."

"I know better."

"Your rational mind, perhaps."

"But you're right. I haven't wanted to be around another woman…until you came. I feel as though someone turned on a light for me and made me look into all the dark corners of my mind. I can see what I've been doing to myself by not accepting her loss." He looked down at Noelle. "You've been that light for me."

"I'm so glad, Bret. You deserve so much happiness. You're a good man, a caring father. It's time for you to accept all the good things that life has to offer."

"Does that include you?"

She looked startled. Carefully she replied, "I'm not certain that I understand what you mean."

"Then you are much too innocent and naive for your own good. Roy knows what's been happening to me. From the way the children made themselves so willingly scarce tonight, I have a hunch they see it, too." He placed a kiss on the tip of her nose, on each cheek, and finally gave her a lingering kiss on the mouth. "I don't want you to disappear out of my life now that I've met you. I want you to stay here with me…with us."

"I'm afraid that won't be possible," she began before he effectively stopped her rebuttal with another long, lingering kiss that seemed to effectively distract her. At least for the moment. Eventually she continued, but on an entirely different subject, he decided. "Christmas season is a magical time, a time when miracles can and often do occur."

He smiled. "I suppose you're right. I feel like I experienced a miracle when you showed up here at the ranch just when we needed you."

"Exactly. I feel very blessed to be here." She stroked his cheek wistfully before she continued. "However, the magic ends on Christmas Day. It reaches its peak at midnight on Christmas Eve. I'll be gone by the next day."

"Nonsense. There's no reason to believe that you can't stay as long as you wish. If you have another job, send them your resignation. Better yet, call and resign now."

"I'm afraid it isn't quite that simple. There are some professions that are considered lifetime callings."

"Perhaps if you explained that—" He paused, realizing what she had just now admitted. "You don't want to stay. That's it, isn't it? You knew when you arrived that you would only be here until Christmas."

"It isn't a question of what I want. It's a question of what I'm allowed to do."

His eyes narrowed. "Are you telling me

that I was right? You're really from some religious order?'' Hastily lifting her off his lap he set her beside him. ''Well, why in the world didn't you say so. How could you let me be kissing and loving you when—''

Her peals of laughter effectively interrupted him. ''No, no. It's nothing like that…well, not exactly. It's just that—'' She paused, resting her head lightly in her palm, thinking. Finally she looked up at him and sighed. ''I really don't know how I can explain. You'll just have to take my word for it that I will only be able to stay until Christmas, then I must go. But we'll be able to enjoy each other during the time I'm here.''

''So you're saying I should accept the miracle of your presence without wanting more.''

''Exactly.''

''Since having you here has made such a tremendous difference in all our lives, I don't suppose I have cause for complaint.'' He stood and pulled her up to stand beside him. ''I'd sound terribly ungrateful not to accept what's been so graciously offered to us.'' He kissed her again before saying, ''It's late. You'd better turn in while I see to the lights and make sure everything's locked up.''

With a slight smile she turned away and left the room. Bret stayed and stared at the tree. The little angel looked tired tonight. Her wand was drooping and her halo had a slight dip in it.

''Patti,'' he whispered, ''you always said I was the most stubborn cuss you'd ever known. I guess you're right. I hung on to your memory for so long, making myself so miserable. The fact is, I almost enjoyed wallowing in my misery. If you'd been here, you would have kicked my rear for acting that way.

''Having Noelle visit has been a miracle, all right. It was like having her hand me a pair of glasses that, once I put them on, made me see what I was doing to myself and the children. You know that I'll never forget you, Patti. I see you in our children every day. We had a wonderful life together. You were my youth.

''I have a chance now to have another life, not better, just different, because I'm different. I know that it'll take some convincing on my part to get Noelle to consider spending her life here on the ranch with me and the children. I don't know how much influence you have on that side, but I'd appreciate it if you'd put in a good word for me.''

He stood there for a long time lost in thought before finally turning off the lights, securing the house and quietly climbing the steps to his empty room.

He wanted to believe in miracles very badly. If this was the reason for them he'd like to apply for one.

Bret fell asleep, thinking of Noelle. Once asleep, he dreamed of her, a normal occurrence for him during the past several nights.

As soon as Noelle woke the next morning, she got up and hurried to the window, knowing that something was different. The ground was covered with a blanket of snow several inches thick. She found the view enchanting. Although it was barely daylight, she hurriedly dressed, found appropriate boots, gloves and a cap, and quietly slipped outside to marvel at the new landscape.

Curiously she touched the snow, awed by

its lightness. Then she scooped some up with her hands and touched it with her tongue. She shivered at the iciness and tossed the snow back to the ground, its cold already coming through her woolen gloves.

She walked toward the barn, then turned and looked at her footprints in the snow. What fun to have experienced Mother Nature's grand performance. The sky continued to lighten and sunlight set the snow to sparkling like the Milky Way on a moonless night...all glittery and shiny, winking and blinking with light and color. No one had ever mentioned bright specks of color in snow...all the colors of the rainbow. Fascinating, simply fascinating.

"Mornin', Miss Noelle," Roy said on his way to the barn from his cabin. "You're up mighty early."

She turned and gave him her version of a sparkling smile. "Oh, yes. When I saw that it had snowed last night, I couldn't wait to come outside and get a closer look."

"Guess you don't get much snow in California." He looked around them and said,

"Even though it means extra work for us here—to make sure the livestock makes it through this cold snap—I've always been kinda partial to days like this. The wind is still so the snow clings to every surface."

Noelle walked over to where he stood and saw how each ordinary ranch implement left outside was now decorated with a trim line of snow. "I imagine the sun will melt it fairly quickly."

"Yes, ma'am."

She started to turn away, then paused. "I need to go start breakfast. You're welcome to join us, you know."

"Thank ya, but I already ate. I might come in for some coffee once I've looked after the animals, though."

Noelle reached the porch in time to meet Bret on his way outside. "What are you doing up so early?"

She laughed. "I couldn't resist getting a closer look at the new snow." He looked so good, standing there in his sheepskin-lined denim jacket, with his Stetson pulled low over his eyes.

He glanced out over the ranch yard, no doubt noting the footprints she and Roy had made, then dropped his gaze down to her. "I'll need to check the rest of the livestock and take hay to them after breakfast. Would you like to come along?"

"I'd like that."

"Good." He touched his forefinger to the curled brim of his hat. "I'll be back in time for breakfast."

When she went inside she discovered that Bret had already started the coffee. Quickly she began to find the necessary ingredients to feed the Bishop clan a warm and nutritious breakfast.

She had just taken the biscuits out of the oven when she heard someone come in. She turned around and saw Travis, still in his pajamas and slippers. He shuffled into the room, still not completely awake.

"Good morning, sleepyhead. How are you this morning?"

He looked at her with wide eyes, his bottom lip quivering. "I had a bad dream," he said in a husky voice.

Noelle immediately walked over and sat down at the table, then beckoned him to join her. When he reached her side, she hoisted him onto her lap and wrapped her arms around him.

He smelled of scented soap and floral shampoo and warm little boy. She hugged him to her and said, "Tell me about your dream, honey."

He sighed and allowed his head to relax against her chest. "I woke up and it was Christmas and there were lots and lots of presents but nobody was there but me. I didn't want to be by myself. It was scary."

"Well, I don't think anything like that will happen to you, sweetie. You've got your daddy, your brother, your sisters and Roy and Freda who all love you and will be around for you so you won't ever have to be alone."

He lifted his head and looked at her. "Will you be here?"

She smiled. "I'm always here for Christmas, remember?"

"On the tree. But I like it better when you're grown-up size and you feed us and things."

"I like it, too, but I won't be able to stay this way. Remember I explained to you about the magic? I'll still be able to talk with you and hear what you tell me each and every year, but I don't think I'll be able to cook for you and look after you."

"Why?"

"Well, eventually I'll have other work... angel kind of work."

"Why can't an angel work in thc kitchen?"

She laughed. "Believe me, Travis, people who work in kitchens and prepare food for others are definitely angels, every one of them." She tried to find words to explain. "You see, I'm a novice angel, which means that I'm learning how to be a full-fledged angel. There's still a lot of things I have to learn, so it's like I'm still going to school."

"You know enough for me. And I want you to stay here and be my mommy."

"Oh, Travis, I know. You told Santa you wanted a mommy for Christmas."

"Yes, but it's you I want, not just any mommy."

"That's the nicest thing anyone has ever

said to me, did you know that? If it were possible, I'd love to stay here and be your mommy. I can't think of anything I'd like better.''

''Can't you be going to angel school while you're being my mommy?''

''I don't think that's quite the way it works.'' She rocked him, wishing she had the wisdom needed to help this little boy. He relaxed against her, content to be in her arms.

The first thing Bret saw when he opened the door was Travis cuddled in Noelle's arms. Her fair head rested against his black curls. Despite the difference in their coloring, they could easily have been mistaken as mother and son. There was so much love shining from each face. Travis looked so contented in Noelle's arms and she looked very natural holding him.

It was one of those moments when everything seemed to come together for Bret. He loved this woman, loved her with a maturity and a passion that almost frightened him. He didn't want to think about what it would mean to let her leave them. He needed her. Travis needed her. The older children did, as well.

Somehow he would have to figure a way to convince her to stay.

He stamped the snow off his boots and came into the kitchen, closing the door behind him. Travis and Noelle looked up at him and smiled, the same trusting innocence shining in each face. Something grabbed at his heart and he was humbled by the love he saw.

Noelle helped Travis off her lap, then went to the stove. "I'll have your eggs for you in a few moments," she said. "Travis and I were chatting and I lost track of the time."

Bret hung his hat and coat on hooks beside the door, then strode over and swung his son up in his arms. "I didn't expect to see you up this early. It seemed like a good morning to stay tucked under the covers for a while."

Travis grinned. "I know."

"As long as you're here, you might as well have breakfast with me and keep me company."

Noelle joined them and they were finishing up when Roy came in. "Thought I'd take you up on that offer of a hot cup of coffee." He took off his leather gloves and briskly rubbed his hands together. "Brrr! Looks like old man winter's getting serious out there."

"I'm taking Noelle with me to check on the rest of the livestock. Do you suppose you can hang around the house for a while, just to keep an eye on things?" His gaze touched Travis before returning to Roy.

"Can't think of anything I'd like more than to build up a big ol' fire in that fireplace. Would ya like to help me, ol' fella?" he asked Travis.

"Can I help carry the wood, too?"

"If you get the right kind of clothes on. Wouldn't want you to get sick this close to Christmas."

Travis slipped away from the table and rushed upstairs. Once he was gone, Roy looked at Bret, glanced at Noelle, then looked back to Bret. "There's something I've been needing to tell you, boss, but I haven't quite known how to bring it up. Seems to me this is as good a time as any."

"That sounds a little ominous, Roy. Don't tell me you're thinking about quitting here, 'cause if you are, I want a chance to convince you otherwise."

Roy grinned. "No. It ain't that. I don't think I'll ever be able to get too far away from your young'uns. They feel like mine."

"Then I'm sure I can handle anything else you might decide to spring on me."

"Well, maybe. Then again..." His slow speech became even slower before he stopped completely, scratching his ear. "I had a little talk with Freda last night after the kids went in to see her. Well, the thing is, I guess I've pretty much taken Freda for granted. I mean, we've known each other for years...been friends and all...but the day she was hurt really got me to thinking. I can't remember a time when I've been so scared. I could see she was in a lot of pain and there wasn't anything I could do for her. That's when it hit me how much Freda means to me. When I got around to telling her how I felt she seemed real surprised—but happy, too—like she felt the same way." He gave Bret a sheepish grin and said, "So there's a good possibility that when Freda returns to the ranch she'll be my wife and live with me."

"I couldn't be happier for you, Roy. I'll admit I'm surprised. I had no idea there was anything in the wind of that nature, but you couldn't do any better than Freda.''

Roy cut his eyes over at Noelle once again before saying to Bret, ''I just thought that you might want to know how things stand and all, in case you were thinking about making plans of your own.''

Bret nodded, biting down hard to keep from smiling. ''That's really decent of you, Roy, keeping my interests in mind like that. I want you to know that I appreciate it.'' He glanced at Noelle. ''I need to get moving. I have quite a lot of ground to cover today.'' Then he smiled innocently.

''Let me clear the table and get my coat. I'll be ready to go in a few minutes.''

The men discussed what needed to be done over the next few days and Noelle cleared the table before going into her room to gather her hastily discarded outerwear. She could feel the pressure building all around her. First the children, then Bret, now Roy. She'd never seen such a transparent bunch of matchmakers in her life.

This wasn't what she'd had in mind when she asked to come into the family to help them during this particular season. She hadn't understood how quickly she would get involved in their lives and heartaches. She hadn't understood how strongly she would grow attached to them.

She hadn't known how deeply she would fall in love with Bret Bishop. Unfortunately there wasn't a thing she could do to remedy the outcome of their present situation.

Chapter Seven

By the time Bret and Noelle reached the gate that would take them off the track to where the cattle were, the sun had melted much of the snow. Only patches dotted the landscape, giving the area a neglected look as though Mother Nature's party was over and everyone had gone home, leaving the remains of the decorations scattered around.

Noelle waited in the warm truck while Bret got out, unlatched the gate, drove through, stopped and relatched it behind them. She looked around but could see no road.

When he crawled back into the truck, she asked, "What happened to the road?"

He grinned. "There won't be a road from now on."

"Then how do you know where to go?"

"Easy. I know every inch of this place. I've learned where I can take a truck." He patted the steering wheel. "It's times like now when this particular horsepower comes in handy." He glanced over at her and winked. "Hang on."

She was glad of the warning. Although Bret seemed to know where he was going, she couldn't see a path anywhere. He drove along an abutment that eventually widened and leveled off.

Once she adjusted to their newest direction, Noelle began to look around, glancing into the brush as they passed. When she saw eyes staring back, she blinked and stared. Adjusting her gaze, she realized that there were deer hidden all around them, watching their progress.

"Bret, look at the deer."

"I know. Why do you think I'm out here?"

"To feed the deer?"

"To make sure there's enough feed for my cattle after the local wildlife eat. It takes a great deal of feed to keep cattle. Some of my ranch acreage has low vegetation and has to be supplemented during certain seasons."

Periodically he would stop the truck to unload hay and grain. He seemed to have a regular route because the cattle would be standing around as though waiting for him to show up.

Noelle found the whole procedure fascinating.

During the last stop, she watched Bret kneel beside a small creek bed and study the ground, frowning. When he joined her once again, his mouth looked grim. He turned the truck in a tight circle and started back the way they'd come.

"Is something wrong?"

"Yeah. It looks like my visitor's back."

"Visitor?"

"Several of the ranchers around here have been complaining of seeing cougar tracks on their property, no doubt stalking the cattle. A few weeks ago, I spent the better part of a day tracking him on my property. The blasted thing crossed my boundaries onto another ranch before I got more than a brief glimpse of his tawny coat. He's a cunning devil.''

''What are you going to do?''

''Saddle Hercules and get back up here as soon as possible. I've got to find that cat before he destroys any of my livestock.''

''Isn't that dangerous?''

''Can be.''

''You'll be careful, won't you?''

He gave her a quick glance from the corner of his eye. ''Are you worrying about me?''

She could feel herself blushing. ''I just want you to be safe.''

He grinned. ''Guess my guardian angel will have to make sure I don't come to any harm.''

''You're teasing me, but I don't care, because you're right. Your guardian angel *will* be with you.''

As soon as they returned to the house Noelle went inside the house. Roy and Travis were in the living room.

''Bret said to tell you he spotted cougar tracks and was going out looking for the cat on horseback.''

Roy shook his head. "Maybe he'll have more luck finding him today than he did last time. Boy, was he ticked off when that cat disappeared onto a neighboring ranch. He said he'd wasted a whole day following him around."

"Isn't it dangerous for him to go out on his own like that?"

"No more than any other time, I reckon. Bret's always careful, though. No need to worry about him." Roy picked up his hat. "Guess I'll see you later, then," he said and walked out of the room.

Noelle turned to Travis. "Would you like to help me bake some cookies?"

"Uh-huh."

"Where are Brenda and Sally?"

"They're upstairs, wrapping presents. They made me promise not to go up until they said I could."

"Is Chris with them?"

"Nope. His friend Jamie wanted him to help move firewood over at his place. He'll be back later."

"How did he get over to Jamie's?"

"Jamie's big brother came and got him."

"Well, then we'll get to work and make up a batch of cookies for everybody."

"Can we make 'em look like Christmas trees and angels and bells and stuff?"

"You bet."

Travis trotted by her side into the kitchen.

Bret saddled Hercules and took off on the road he and Noelle had just followed. He knew he needed to take care of the cougar, but what he wanted to do was to stay at the house with Noelle. He wanted to spend as much time as possible with her. Somehow he needed to convince her that they could work out whatever was going on with her. She was obviously a very loyal person. He couldn't fault that. Loyalty was an admirable trait.

He would just have to convince her that he deserved her loyalty as well as her present employer. He smiled to himself, thinking of all the ways he would enjoy convincing her that she needed to stay with the Bishop family.

Once he left the main road, he took the horse directly to the last sighting he'd had of the cougar's tracks, rather than following the trail made by the truck. There were times when traveling by horseback could save him miles. This was one of those times.

Dismounting, he knelt and studied the tracks, then circled the watering hole for any sign. When he came across tracks leading into the rugged hills, he remounted and slowly followed them, keeping his eyes trained on the surrounding foliage, as well.

Despite his focus on the cat tracks, Bret lost some of his concentration because he kept thinking about Noelle. The unexpected whirr of the deadly rattlesnake spooked the horse as well as startling Bret. He'd been leaning forward, peering up into the trees for a possible sighting of tawny fur when the horse let out a snort and began to buck.

Feeling like a complete fool for having been caught unprepared like some greenhorn, Bret had only an instant to realize that he wasn't going to be able to stay in the saddle. The world did a crazy tilt as he sailed over the horse's head. Bret concentrated on relaxing and rolling with the fall.

It wouldn't be the first time he'd been forcibly ejected from a saddle, he managed to think before he came to an abrupt halt as he slammed against the hard ground on his back.

He would have been all right except for some bruising if he hadn't fallen beside a granite upcropping. The jagged ridge of rock caught him behind the ear as his head whipped back from the fall.

One instant he was aware of a whirling blue sky, the next instant pain exploded in his head, turning the blue sky into a fathomless darkness.

By midafternoon Noelle could not keep her eyes away from the kitchen window that overlooked the direction Bret had taken a few hours before. There was still no sign of him. Shouldn't he have found the cougar by now?

She was alone in the kitchen. Travis was upstairs taking his nap, the girls had gone to visit with friends and Chris had returned home to help Roy somewhere on the ranch.

She couldn't quite forget the shiver that had raced over her when she'd watched from this same window as Bret had ridden away earlier. She'd seen him leave the house alone on several occasions before today. She couldn't understand her uneasiness when she'd watched his solitary figure ride out.

The girls returned in time for a late lunch. She fed them and they disappeared upstairs. When she went to check on Travis he was still sound asleep, Rex curled up on the rug beside his bed. Once again she fought her uneasiness. Rex was usually by Bret's side. Perhaps his staying behind was what made the day seem different to her.

Noelle tiptoed over and adjusted Travis's cover before she left the room.

Next, she went into her bedroom and checked the kittens, smiling as they milled around on wobbly legs, batting at each other, their eyes barely opened. She sat back on her heels, remembering how Bret had been so badly outnumbered on the question of whether or not to keep the kittens or to attempt to give them away. All four were now officially members of the Bishop family, each with its own name and owner.

She had a hunch that none of them would be sleeping in the barn.

Noelle returned to the kitchen and peered out the window once again. She couldn't quite shake her restlessness. Her thoughts kept returning to Bret and how lonely he'd looked riding off alone. A brief picture of him flashed into her mind and she froze, frightened. She saw him lying on the ground, his eyes closed, his face almost gray. Hercules stood nearby, restlessly shaking his head. She could almost hear the whuffling sound of the horse and the jingle of the bridle.

Had something happened to Bret?

Unable to stay in the house another moment, she grabbed her coat off the hook and slipped it on, then stepped outside on the porch. The wind had picked up since morning, and it felt icy whipping around the corner of the house.

Worried, she peered up the lane where he'd gone, but she could see nothing.

She was still standing outside when Roy and Chris drove into the yard in the truck. Giving in to impulse, Noelle went over to the truck.

"Howdy," Roy said, opening the door. "It's a little cold to be standing around outside, ain't it?"

"Roy, I'm worried about Bret."

He glanced around. "Where is he?"

"He left several hours ago to check out those cougar tracks. I haven't seen him since then."

Roy pushed his hat back and scratched his head. "Well, there's nothing unusual about that. A man can spend hours trailing that cat. Bret's been worried about the cussed thing. He's probably decided not to come home until he gets him."

"But what if he's hurt…or something?"

Roy gave her a sharp look. "Whaddaya mean?"

She bit her bottom lip and looked away. Meanwhile Chris had walked around the truck and joined them. He stood there watching her, his gaze intent on her face. She forced herself to look at Chris, to let him see her concern. His face blanched but he showed no other sign.

"Let's go find him, Roy," Chris said quietly.

"Well, son, I can't see where we need to—"

"I do. I think Noelle's right. We need to go find Dad."

Roy looked from one to the other with uneasiness written on his face.

"If you think we should, Chris, of course we'll go. I just didn't want your dad irritated at us for wasting time."

"He'll understand," was all Chris said, turning away. Then he stopped and looked back at Noelle. He touched her lightly on the shoulder. "He's okay, isn't he?"

She heard the frightened little boy beneath the young man's calm. She closed her eyes, forcing herself not to alarm him more than she already had. On a subconscious level Chris remembered her, remembered who she was, remembered their talks so long ago. She had consciously touched the bond that had been forged between them without fully stopping to think how it would affect him.

"You'll find him," she whispered, nodding. "That's the important thing."

"Did he take Rex with him?"

"No. Rex is upstairs with Travis."

Chris hurried into the house. Within minutes he reappeared with Rex. The dog sniffed the wind, then looked up at Chris. Chris lowered the tailgate of the truck and Rex leaped inside.

Chris crawled into the cab of the truck and said, "Let's go, Roy."

Noelle briefly described to Roy where she and Bret had gone that morning to save Roy and Chris as much time as possible. She stood in the middle of the ranch yard for a long time after they had disappeared from view, praying that they found him before dark, praying that he was all right.

Then she turned and slowly went into the house for the long wait ahead of her.

When she heard the faint sound of a vehicle coming down the lane what seemed to be hours later, Noelle rushed to the door. The rest of the children had been fed and were upstairs. She had explained to them that Roy and Chris had gone to look for Bret, that she was certain he was all right, but that she felt he needed some assistance.

Because she was calm, they were calm.

Their trust in her touched her like nothing ever had.

She slipped outside and was waiting on the porch when the truck stopped a few feet away. The gray gloom of late afternoon had sunk into deep shadows. All she could make out was that Rex wasn't alone in the bed of the pickup truck.

Roy hopped out of the cab of the truck and hurried to the back. She followed. "Is he all right?"

"Yeah, I think so. A little groggy, but he recognized us. Last thing he remembered was flying off that blamed horse. He must have hit his head on something. He's got a he—a heck of a knot behind his ear."

Chris had been sitting in the back, allowing his dad to rest against him. Between Roy and Chris they managed to help Bret off the truck.

She could no longer stay away from him. Moving closer, she ran her hands over his face and shoulders. "Bret?"

"I'm okay," he growled in disgust, then promptly made a liar of himself when his knees buckled. Roy and Chris each took an arm and helped him up the front steps.

"Put him in my room. It's closest," she said, running ahead of them and holding the door open.

Bret began to protest but Roy interrupted with, "Don't be a fool, boss. There's no reason for you to climb those steps right now."

As soon as she saw him in the kitchen light she knew that Bret was in pain. His skin was a pasty white and he kept shivering. She hurried into her room and pulled back the covers. She looked at Roy and said, "Help him get out of those cold clothes. I'll make him something hot to drink."

Roy nodded. "Good idea." He looked at Chris. "To be on the safe side, I want you to call Dr. Warner. Have him—"

"No!" Bret said, then winced at the sound. Ruefully he rubbed his head as though apologizing for the noise. "I'll be all right, once I get warm and have something hot inside me."

"I'm sure you will, but I want Warner to look at your head, maybe check your ribs, anyway. It's either that, or I'm hauling you into town, myself. You decide."

Bret stared at Roy for a moment and realized that this was going to be one argument he was going to lose. He sighed. "Do what you want," he replied.

Chris left the room and Roy pulled off Bret's heavy jacket, then eased him to the side of the bed. He methodically pulled off his boots and reached for his belt. "I'm not completely helpless, dammit," Bret growled, pushing Roy's hands away. He stood, swaying, unfastened his jeans and slid them over his hips.

Bret pulled off his shirt and stretched out on the bed. Roy pulled the covers up, found another blanket and added it to the bed. Rex, who had followed them inside the house, lay his head on the side of the bed and looked at Bret in concern.

Noelle returned carrying a large mug of hot liquid. Chris was immediately behind her. She sat down on the edge of the bed and held out the cup.

"Dr. Warner said I was lucky to catch him," Chris said, standing at the end of the bed. "He was on his way out the door. He said he would be right on out here...before he made any other stops."

"It's a waste of his time," Bret muttered, then sipped the reviving tea. He grudgingly admitted to himself that Roy might have a point. He felt very strange at the moment, not to mention humiliated. He couldn't remember the last time he'd been thrown off his horse!

"Did someone bring in Hercules?" he asked, looking up at Roy.

"I'll make sure he gets put away properly. I tied the reins to the saddle. He'll follow us in."

Bret closed his eyes. "Make sure he does." He didn't remember Noelle taking the cup from him.

The next thing he knew Dr. Warner was poking and prodding him. "Ow, Doc," he murmured, feeling probing fingers along his ribs.

"Yeah, I thought so," Dr. Warner replied. "We better tape up these ribs, just in case you may have cracked them."

Roy stood in the door. "Think we should take him to the hospital for X rays?"

Before Bret could protest, Dr. Warner was shaking his head. "There's no need to make him travel that far for tests. The hospital's full. We'd have to send him back home again." He looked up at Noelle. "Don't believe we've met."

"No, sir. I'm Noelle St. Nichols."

The doctor grinned. "Pleased to make your acquaintance. Hope you don't mind filling in for a couple of days looking after this character. He needs to stay in bed and let those ribs rest. He's got a mild concussion, and from the looks of things he spent a little too much time lying around outdoors in this kind of weather." He peered at her over the top of his glasses and she knew he wanted her to understand the seriousness of the situation.

She nodded. "I'll look after him."

"Good." He stood and stepped away from the bed. "I'll give you something to help with his aches and pains. I want you to monitor his temperature. If it starts to climb, call me right away. You got that?"

"Yes, sir."

He smiled. "He's tough, you know. He's gotten banged up a lot more than this since I've known him."

"You keep talking about me like I'm not even here," Bret complained. Noelle looked down at him and smiled. He felt his heart contract at the sweetness of her look. "Are the kids all right?"

She nodded. "Worried about you."

"Tell 'em I'm all right."

"I will."

He looked around the room. "Guess you'll have to sleep upstairs for tonight."

"I don't mind."

The doctor nodded. "I'll give you a call in the morning." Once again he looked at Noelle. "Call me if there are any changes."

"You can count on it."

Bret kept dozing off, so that the time seemed to be moving in jerky, freeze-frame motion. He was alone, then Noelle was there. He was alone, then all four children were there. He'd close his eyes for just a moment, and when he would open them he would be alone once again.

Roy was there. Then he wasn't. He heard voices in the kitchen. Then it was quiet. Chris came in to report that Hercules was safe, dry and fed. Roy mentioned he was going to the hospital to see Freda. He heard the shower going upstairs, footsteps on the stairs, Noelle's voice talking to the children. With a deep sigh, he let go and allowed himself to drift away.

The next time he opened his eyes the house was quiet and the room was dark, except for a tiny night-light glowing from the adjoining bathroom. For a moment, Bret couldn't figure out where he was. Then he remembered.

He'd gone looking for the cougar... Hercules got spooked...he'd been thrown off. He could feel the pain in his ribs as well as his head. If only his head—

"Here. The doctor said this should help the pain."

Bret opened his eyes and looked up. Noelle stood beside the bed, holding a glass and a capsule. He blinked, then rubbed his eyes. It *was* Noelle, wasn't it?

Absently he took the capsule and swallowed it without taking his eyes off the woman who stood beside the bed. He couldn't have taken his eyes off her if his life depended on it.

She glowed. There was no other term for it.

She wore a white robe and her hair was loose around her shoulders. Just above her head was a pulsating, circular light that looked remarkably like a halo. Just past her shoulders he could see the gauzy outline of wings, giant wings that looked capable of lifting her.

"Noelle?" His voice didn't work. He licked his lips and tried again.

"I'm right here, Bret. Try to rest. Dr. Warner said you should be feeling much better by morning."

"Travis was right," he managed to say. "You *are* an angel." He could feel his pulse begin to race and his heart pound.

She nodded.

"I'm not dreaming this, am I?"

"No."

"What are you doing here?"

"Looking after you…and your family."

"I know. What I mean is…you aren't real, are you?"

She smiled. "Of course I'm real."

He reached out and brushed his fingers along her sleeve. She took his hand and held it between both of hers. He had difficulty swallowing. "All those things you said…about other commitments. You're not able to stay here because you're a— You're a—an—"

"That's right. I'm so glad you understand. I didn't like the idea of misleading you about me."

"Understand? How can I understand? This isn't possible." He closed his eyes, opened them, saw she was still there and closed them again. They remained closed. "I know what it is. I have a concussion. The doctor said so. I'm probably delirious. I'm dreaming this whole conversation." He opened his eyes.

Noelle stood beside him in her nightclothes, still holding the empty glass he'd drunk from earlier. The night-light cast a soft glow around her. There was no sign of either a halo or wings.

"How are you feeling?" she asked, placing her palm on his forehead.

"Like I'm losing my mind," he admitted, as though to himself. "I can't tell when I'm awake or asleep."

"It's probably the medication. Don't fight it. Just allow it to work so that you can rest."

His eyes drifted shut. He needed his rest. He was obviously overtired or he would never have dreamed such an impossible scene. Travis's stories about angels had finally gotten to him.

Chapter Eight

Bret opened his eyes and realized that from the light in the room he'd overslept. Again. In the days since his mishap he'd spent more time asleep than awake.

After the first night, he'd been sleeping in his own room. After that memorable night, he hadn't done any more hallucinating about Noelle.

Thank God.

He lay there for a moment, listening. The house was silent of voices, which was unusual in his household. He wondered where the children were. After all, today was Christmas Eve. They were bound to be excited and full of eager energy.

Moving gingerly, he got up and went into the bathroom.

Dr. Warner had come out yesterday and cut off the tape around his chest, but only after extracting a promise from Bret that he wouldn't be doing any heavy lifting.

Now Bret looked into the mirror at his bruised ribs. At least now he could stand under the shower to bathe instead of having to wash around his bandages. The water felt good and he stood there for countless minutes, enjoying the soothing massage.

He also took his time shaving and dressing, refusing to admit to himself that he wasn't looking forward to going downstairs to what he suspected was an empty house.

Over the years he'd sometimes wondered how he would feel to be alone again... completely alone. Sometimes when the kids were fighting with each other, or one of them was sick, or a teacher called with a stern request for a conference, he'd wondered what his life would be like without a family.

This morning he had an uneasy feeling, as though he'd awakened in a different space and time. As though he was now living another kind of life altogether, where he'd never married, or had children—a life where he had chosen to be alone.

That blow on the head had really done a number on his thinking processes.

Bret patted after-shave on his face, dried his hands and headed downstairs. He paused when he reached the bottom of the steps and looked into the living room.

Lights twinkled on the tree. Everything in the room—from the floor to the furniture—had a shimmering glow about it. He walked over to the fireplace, where a fire danced with twists of flame.

Someone had decided to move the kittens in closer to the warmth of the fire. Mischief was curled up asleep in the basket that had been made into her bed. Four tiny balls of fur were curled into a pile of multicolored fluff.

He smiled to himself, remembering the argument he'd lost regarding the latest arrivals. Christmas kittens, he'd been told, were very special and needed to be treated with respect.

After a moment he went across the hall and into the kitchen. Something was baking in the oven—bread, perhaps—giving the room a wonderful scent. He heard a slight noise from the bedroom off the kitchen.

"Noelle?"

She appeared in the doorway. "Oh! I didn't hear you stirring. You must be hungry." She started toward the refrigerator until he stopped her with a light touch on her shoulder.

"I'm okay. Where is everybody?"

"Roy invited the children to go with him to see Freda. She's leaving the hospital today. He's planning to drive her to Austin to be with her sister. He promised the children that they could come."

"When did they leave?"

"Not quite an hour ago."

He glanced outside. The sun shone brightly. "Doesn't look as though they're going to have the snow they wanted."

"No."

He walked over to the window and peered out, his hands in his back pockets. Noelle looked at his back for a moment before turning away and finding the ingredients for his breakfast. Soon she had bacon frying, eggs on the griddle and bread in the toaster. She poured him a cup of coffee.

"Is something wrong?" she asked in the continued silence.

He turned away from the window and looked at her. "I suppose you're leaving today, aren't you?"

Suddenly she was busy scooping up the eggs, draining the bacon and buttering the toast. "That's right."

"Is there anything I can say or do to make you change your mind?"

She shook her head without looking up.

He sighed and sat down at the table. Methodically he ate the food in front of him, not really tasting it. When he was through, he said, "It's hard to realize that you've been here two weeks. In some ways, I feel as though I've known you forever. In others, I can't believe two weeks have gone by since you arrived."

She sat down across from him and clasped her hands. "I've enjoyed being here. You have a warm, loving family."

"They deserve so much more than I've given them."

"You've given them love. You've been there whenever they needed you."

"I've been selfish, wrapped up in my own pain." His eyes met hers. "You've taught me that."

He pushed away from the table. "I want to check on the animals. Do you need a ride over to Ida's?"

She shook her head.

"Have you already told the kids goodbye?"

"Not yet, but they understand that I have to leave."

He pulled his jacket on and reached for his hat. "Guess there isn't much more to say then…except to thank you for looking after all of us. I wish you the best of everything."

"Bret?"

"What?"

"I'll be here until late tonight. At least we can enjoy what time there is together."

He stiffened. "What do you mean?"

She smiled. "If you're leaving you could give me a kiss goodbye."

Her request obviously startled him. She saw him tense, his face showing no expression. "Sure," he muttered in an offhanded manner.

She came to him, went up on her toes and kissed him sweetly. He stood there, willing himself not to grab her and beg. Her hands rested on his chest. He could feel their imprint burning a brand on him. When she pulled away, her eyes were brimming with unshed tears.

"Please be happy," she whispered.

He fought for control of his emotions. He swallowed hard, then nodded. "You, too." He jammed his hat on his head, opened the door and stepped outside.

The sun had fooled him. The air was much colder than he'd expected. He took several deep breaths, willing away the emotion that had threatened to overcome him. He'd managed this far in his life without Noelle. There was no reason to believe he couldn't continue.

After he was finished outside, Bret decided to ride into town and have coffee with some of the other ranchers. He was glad he did because he got some good news. They'd managed to catch the cougar that had been prowling around the countryside. One of the officials from an exotic ranch in the area had shown up and offered to trap the cat and release it in a less populated area.

Bret enjoyed visiting with his friends and neighbors. He felt as though he was seeing them with new eyes. They were a friendly bunch who had made many overtures toward him these past few years to join in their social life. They'd never given up on him, even when he'd been his most surly.

He wasn't sure what had changed his perspective, but he knew that he was looking at his life and the people around him in a new way.

"The family all ready for Christmas?" one of the ranchers asked.

"More than ready," Bret replied.

"Your family sure has seen its share of problems this year, Bishop," another said. "I understand Freda's leaving the hospital today."

"Yes. Roy and the children went to help her get moved."

"I must say you're looking good, considering your mishap."

"I wasn't hurt badly, except for my pride," he admitted.

Everyone laughed.

Nobody asked him about Noelle and he felt reluctant to bring her into the conversation. None of them knew her, anyway, so it didn't really matter.

He was getting into his truck when he spotted a familiar face leaving the post office. On an impulse, Bret decided to go say hello to Ida Schulz.

She was getting into her car when he reached her side.

"Hi, Ida. It's good to see you."

She glanced around in surprise. "Well, hello, Bret. I haven't seen you in a long while. How's Freda?"

"Doing well. She's getting out of the hospital today. Roy and the kids are taking her over to her sister's in Austin. I think they're planning a little celebration for her over there."

"I'm sure she'll appreciate it." She got into

the car and closed the door, rolling down the window.

Bret leaned over and said, "I haven't taken the time to thank you for sending your niece out to help when—"

Ida looked at him in surprise. "My what?"

"Your niece... N—"

"You must be mistaken, Bret. I don't have a niece."

He stared at her. "You don't?"

"I've got two nephews, though. They live over near Killeen. My brother's boys."

"No niece," he repeated slowly.

"Nope. Ed was always sorry they didn't have a girl, of course." She looked at her watch. "I hate to rush off like this, Bret, but I've got some more errands to run, plus company coming in and all." She started the car. "You be sure to tell Freda hello for me. Hope she's continuing to improve."

Bret stood there and watched as she pulled out of the parking space, his mind whirling.

Noelle wasn't Ida Schulz's niece, because Ida Schulz didn't have a niece.

Then who in the world was Noelle St. Nichols?

A sudden memory shook him, a memory of the night he had banged his head. She had come to him and she had—

No. There wasn't any way. She couldn't be.

He went back to his truck and started home. He now knew who she wasn't. He was going to find out who she was before the day was over. He wanted some answers.

Bret opened the back door and stepped into the empty kitchen, looking around him. Cakes, pies, cookies and homemade candy lined one of the cabinets. There was enough food there to feed the entire county.

He removed his jacket, hung it beside his hat and continued into the hallway.

He found Noelle in the living room and for a moment could only stare at the scene before him.

She sat on the rug in front of the fire with Rex curled up beside her on one side, Mischief on the other. Mischief eyed the dog from time to time but for the most part she ignored him, instead keeping her attention on the kittens who were venturing out of their basket and exploring their immediate world.

Rex sniffed at one, then blinked when it hissed and turned into a bristling fur ball.

Bret's gaze went from the woman with a soft smile watching the kittens to the tree that sparkled nearby. The little angel on top looked almost new. Her dress was starched and stood away from her, her hair fell in soft waves and curls, looking freshly combed and her wings glimmered in the light.

When he looked back at Noelle she was watching him, waiting.

He walked into the room and sat in his favorite chair before the fire. Rex pushed himself up and came over to him, shoving his nose beneath Bret's hand.

Noelle continued to watch him. She wore the same soft smile on her face she'd had with the animals.

Absently Bret rubbed Rex's ears, wondering what to say…how to begin.

"You aren't Ida Schulz's niece," he finally said in a statement more than a question.

"No," she agreed quietly.

"I want to know who you are."

She tilted her head. "Do you?" There was a hint of doubt in her voice.

"Of course!" he replied with exasperation. "There was no reason to lie to me. You could have just said that you—" He paused, running his hand through his hair, feeling more than a little foolish. "Well, you could have told me the truth—whatever it is. You were passing through town...needed a job...heard about Freda...whatever happened, you could have told me."

She shifted so that she was facing him, her knees pulled up to her chin. "I think that you've always known who I am, Bret, but you couldn't admit it, at least not to yourself...especially not to yourself."

"Now wait a minute. You aren't going to start in with that—" he waved his hand toward the tree "—Christmas tree angel stuff, I hope. I'll admit that you look like her, and I can see where the kids would think that you had come to help us and all, but—"

"But you don't believe in angels."

"Of course not."

"And therefore I can't be an angel."

"Exactly."

"Then who am I?"

He leaned forward in his chair, his elbows resting on his knees. "How should I know? I haven't been able to figure out how you got into the house in the first place. I told myself that Chris forgot to lock the door, but he never forgets something like that. You said someone brought you but there were no tire tracks outside and with the rain that blew in, the ground was soft enough to leave tracks. The only ones I saw were the ones Roy made when he and Chris came home."

"Why haven't you said something before?"

He shook his head in bewilderment. "I don't know. I guess everything was happening at once and I was having trouble keeping up with all the changes. I remember thinking that you must have walked, but you were dry. Besides, that suitcase would have weighed too much for you to have hauled it any distance at all."

"An angel could do all of those things, Bret. Appear without getting wet, manifest a suitcase filled with appropriate clothes..."

"But angels aren't *real*, Noelle, can't you understand that? They're just something people make up to help deal with their own fears about life.''

Noelle gracefully unfolded her legs and came to kneel between his knees. ''I'm real, Bret, for the next few hours, I'm very real.''

This close he could see the love in her eyes, as well as the compassion and understanding. He felt as though everything he knew about himself, his life and reality was being questioned and tested.

With a groan he pulled her into his arms, cuddling her to him, holding her in such a firm grip that no one would be able to take her from him. ''Don't go,'' he whispered, burying his face against her neck, ''I don't care who you are, or why you came. I just know that I need you in my life.'' He found her lips and kissed her, putting all of his feelings and yearnings into the kiss.

She twined her arms around his neck, kissing him back, refusing to think of anything more than this moment.

They heard Roy's truck and knew that the children had returned home. ''I'm going to stay out of the way for the rest of the afternoon,'' she whispered. ''This is your time with the children. Once they're in bed I'll spend my last hours with you.''

Before he could protest, she slipped off his lap. He heard the door to Freda's room close just before the children burst into the house.

The children were filled with enthusiasm. They had stories to tell about Freda and the party her sister had for her. They excitedly showed Bret the gifts they'd gotten to open while they were there and how pleased Freda was with what they had given her.

For the rest of the afternoon and early evening, Bret kept busy with the children. They all trooped outside to feed the animals their special Christmas Eve meals, and Chris pointed out to Travis the stars that Santa used to navigate on his flight from the North Pole. When they returned inside Bret found the CD of Christmas songs he'd bought in San Antonio. He played it and the children sang along with gusto.

Chris and Sally coaxed Travis upstairs to take his bath and to get ready for bed while Brenda helped Bret to get the stockings to be hung near the fireplace ready for Santa's visit.

"Could I help fill them, Daddy?" she asked.

He grinned. "And ruin Santa's fun? No way."

"Ah, Daddy. I know it's you."

He sat down on the sofa and hugged her. "Don't you ever get too old to believe in Santa, honey. He's as real as you and me."

"Really? Then he's like Noelle? He can really come and visit on Christmas, even though he's just an angel or spirit or something?"

Bret grew still as he looked at his oldest daughter. "Is that what Noelle did?"

She frowned. "Well, sure. That's what she said."

"When was that?"

"The first day she was here. She explained that she would only be able to stay until Christmas."

"So that's why no one is surprised that she's leaving."

Brenda smiled. "She won't be *gone,* Daddy." She pointed. "She'll be right there." She looked up and smiled at the angel. "She made this year's Christmas extra special, didn't she?"

"Yes, honey. Very special." He looked around the room, avoiding her gaze. "You'd better get to bed, yourself."

Brenda gave Bret a hug. "Good night, Daddy. Merry Christmas."

"Merry Christmas, baby," he replied.

He followed her upstairs, told Travis a long, involved story that eventually put him sound asleep, peeked in at the girls, then paused in Chris's doorway.

His son was in bed with earphones on. When he saw his dad, he pulled off the headset and shut off the radio. "It's a little early for me to go to sleep," he explained with a grin.

"I know. I'm surprised that Brenda and Sally are already asleep."

"Well, they had a full day, helping with Freda and all. It was kind of fun, like Freda and her family are a part of our family."

"Has Roy mentioned how long Freda intends to stay in Austin?"

Chris grinned. "If Roy has his way, he's going to haul her off to get married as soon as Christmas is over."

"So he's told you about his plans, has he?"

"Yeah, but he didn't have to. I mean, a blind man could have figured out what was going on with him. You should have seen him the day Freda fell. You would have thought he'd caused the accident on purpose."

Bret leaned against the doorjamb. "I'm glad they've admitted how they feel."

"Me, too." He cleared his throat. "Speaking of feelings, Dad. Your feelings for Noelle have been fairly obvious. Did you mention to her how you felt about her?"

"I tried, but it didn't do much good. For whatever reasons, she's made it clear she couldn't stay around here. Besides, why would she want to?"

"Maybe because she loves you…and us, too."

Bret tilted his head slightly and looked at his son. "Aren't you going to try to convince me that Noelle isn't really Ida Schulz's niece? That she's an angel?"

Chris's gaze remained steady. "Why should I do a thing like that?"

"Well, I'm glad there's somebody in this family who isn't caught up in all this Christmas magic stuff. I was beginning to think I'd lost my mind.''

''All I'm saying is that I think you should have told her how you felt.''

''I asked her to stay.''

''That isn't the same thing as telling her how you feel.''

''Sure it is. I want her around.''

''Why?''

''Because.''

''Because, why?''

Bret could feel his frustration grow. He used to have these kinds of conversations with Chris when he was Travis's age. He counted to ten in silence before he said, ''This is a pointless conversation. I'll talk to you in the morning.''

''Why don't you want to admit that you love her, Dad? There's nothing wrong with that, you know. Admitting how you feel might make all the difference in the world.''

''Good night, Chris,'' Bret said, straightening.

''Good night, Dad,'' Chris cheerfully replied. ''Merry Christmas.''

"Smart-alec kid," Bret muttered to himself, returning downstairs. He had enough to keep him busy tonight without listening to Chris's crackpot advice.

He pulled a set of keys off one of the hooks in the kitchen and went over to Roy's cabin. Roy had already told him he wouldn't be back tonight. As he had done every year, Bret had stored the gifts he set out beneath the tree at Roy's place, where the children wouldn't find them. He let himself into the place, gathered up the boxes, and returned to the house, quietly letting himself back in.

He found Noelle waiting for him. She took some of the presents and helped to arrange them around the tree, then helped him fill the long red felt stockings with fruit, nuts and candy.

"Thank you for helping me," he said when they were through.

"I enjoyed it."

He took her hand and led her to the sofa, then sat down beside her. "Would it make a difference to your leaving if I told you how much I love you, Noelle?" he asked. "I want to marry you," he finally admitted aloud.

Tears made her eyes shine, reflecting the lights from the tree. "There is nothing I would like more, Bret, but I don't have that choice. I have to leave at midnight."

"How? How can you leave? Do you expect me to take you somewhere? Or do you have someone coming to pick you up?"

"No. I'll leave the way I came." She smiled with a hint of sadness. "In a blink of an eye...now you see me...now you don't."

"Like an angel."

"Yes."

He sighed. "This isn't funny, Noelle."

"I know."

"I'm not a child."

"You've forgotten the wisdom of childhood. You've forgotten how to believe."

He lifted his brows incredulously. "You mean you would stay if I'd believe you were an angel? Is this some kind of test?"

"I don't have any control over getting to stay, Bret. I would stay if I could, believe me. There's nothing more I could want than to spend a lifetime with you and the children." She leaned her head against his shoulder. "It's just that I have other commitments that I must honor.''

''My loving you doesn't matter, is that it?''

''Your loving me is the greatest gift I could receive.''

''Will you ever come back?''

''I don't know. If possible, I'd like to come back.''

He glanced up to the top of the tree. ''At Christmas?''

''Perhaps. We'll see.''

He pulled a small package out of his pocket. ''Here's something I want you to have,'' he said, offering the gaily wrapped gift to her.

Her eyes had misted over so much that Noelle was having trouble seeing. When she finally managed to open the gift she felt the lump in her throat grow. A heart locket hung on a thin gold chain. She opened it and found a picture of Bret on one side and a picture of the children on the other.

''I know it sounds corny to say, but I want you to carry the thought of us in your heart, no matter where you go.''

Tears trickled down her cheeks. ''I love

you, Bret Bishop. I love you with all my heart. If there was any way I could, I would stay here with you. I would be your wife and love and cherish your children…if I could.''

Her sincerity and her pain were too obvious to doubt. He could only nod.

She kissed him with love and longing, with an almost desperate intensity, until the almost silent chiming of the mantel clock called them both back to the present…and reality.

With a final kiss she broke away from him. ''Goodbye, my love. God bless you.''

One moment he had his arms around her, the next moment he was alone in the room, wondering what had happened. Had he been sleeping? Was he awake even now?

Bret looked around the room. The tree still sparkled with light, music played in the background, presents were piled high all around it, long, red felt stockings were stuffed for each child and the tiny angel at the top of the tree watched him with compassion.

He shook his head, got up and went all through the house. Each child was asleep, the cat and her kittens were down for the count, even Rex merely opened one eye before shutting it with a sigh.

Freda's bedroom was neat and orderly, and unoccupied.

The refrigerator and pantry were stocked full of food for the next day. Everything was ready for Christmas.

Only one change had taken place…Noelle was gone.

Bret knew he needed to go upstairs to try to get some sleep. The children would be up by dawn, insisting on getting him downstairs to open gifts.

However, Bret returned to the living room knowing this was one night when he'd be unable to sleep. Instead, he went into the kitchen and made coffee, then found a bottle of brandy and carried them into the living room. He sat down on the sofa, so that he could look at the tree and the angel at the top.

He didn't understand what had happened but he did understand the miracle that had occurred in his own heart. Somehow his appreciation of life had been given back to him. For the first time in over three years, he felt whole again.

The music played softly in the background. The scent of vanilla and cinnamon and bayberry filled the air. The only light in the room came from the tree. He leaned back, took a deep breath and relaxed. Occasionally he sipped on his coffee, enjoying the blend of flavors, and absorbed the sights, scents and celebration of this time of year.

In the quiet of the night, on this very special night, Bret acknowledged to himself how much Noelle had given to him. He would always love her.

He relived the times they had spent together...the mall in San Antonio, dinner along the river. He remembered all that she had told him.

Once again he looked up at the tree. "If there's such a thing as Christmas magic, then I ask that Noelle be returned to us, that we be given the opportunity to live together and to love together."

His eyes blurred and he closed them, wiping the unexpected moisture away. He was really losing his grip on reality, sitting there talking to himself as though there really was a Santa, a Christmas angel, a magical time of year.

Bret set his cup down and rested his head against the back of the sofa, knowing he needed to get some sleep. The kids would be up early in the morning, eager to—

He felt something brush against his hand. No doubt Mischief had decided to look for some attention. Lazily he opened his eyes— and stared in disbelief.

A brilliant light filled the room, almost blinding him. He blinked a couple of times before he could see anything. The light seemed to be centered immediately in front of him.

He felt more than heard a voice say, *"You may not believe in us, but we believe in you. We have done what we could to protect and guide you. Now you ask that one of us join you in your dimension, giving up her studies with us. This is highly unorthodox, but because she is willing to forgo her training with us at this time, we allow the choice to be hers."*

The light gradually diminished until the tiny lights of the tree were all that illuminated the living room. Bret stared at his cup of coffee, wondering how much brandy he'd put in there.

What was the matter with him? Had he fallen asleep? He looked around the room. The kittens were asleep in their basket. He didn't know where Mischief was.

Bret forced himself to get up, turn off the lights, and go upstairs.

Maybe he'd better have Dr. Warner take a look at him the next time he was in town. His eyes and his hearing were definitely acting up on him.

Chapter Nine

He'd just closed his eyes, or so it seemed, when the door to his bedroom opened and the whispers and giggles moved to the side of his bed.

"Dad! C'mon, it's time to get up. It's time to open our presents!"

Bret squinted through swollen eyelids at Travis and sighed. Of course it was time. It certainly wasn't Travis's fault that his dad seemed to be having some kind of a hallucinatory midlife crisis.

With a groan Bret sat up and looked at Sally

and Brenda, hovering nearby. "Did you wake him up?" he growled.

Brenda giggled. "No. He woke *us* up."

"Figures," Bret muttered. "All right. Give me a minute and I'll be downstairs."

As soon as they left he threw the covers back and went into the bathroom. After splashing water over his face several times he returned to the bedroom and got dressed. He didn't take time to shower or shave. He could do that after the kids enjoyed the results of all these weeks of anticipation.

He was the last one downstairs. Out of habit he turned on the tree lights and glanced up at the top.

The angel was gone. Before he could register the shock he felt, Travis said, "What happened to Noelle?"

The other three children looked up and gasped. Instead of an angel, a bright star glowed at the top of the tree, as though lit from inside.

Sally jumped up. "What did you do with her?" she demanded to know of her father.

Brenda said, "Dad, how could you?"

Chris said, "I don't understand."

Bret exchanged a glance with his bewildered son. "*You* don't understand! Believe me, neither do I!"

A tinkling chuckle caught their attention. They all turned to the hallway and gaped at the young woman standing there. She walked into the room, smiling. "It's simple, really. The angel is gone." She smiled at each of them, but her gaze lingered on Bret. "I hope you don't mind if I'm here to take her place."

"Noelle?" Chris asked, his adolescent voice cracking halfway through her name.

She nodded. "Yes."

Travis threw himself at her, his arms clutched around her waist. "You didn't go away. You stayed here!"

Her gaze stayed steady as she continued to look at Bret. "If you still want me, I can stay here."

If he was dreaming, Bret didn't ever want to wake up. The fact that his children also saw her reassured him tremendously. He paused in front of her, unable to stop grinning. Taking her hand in his, he said, "You came back."

"Yes."

"How?"

"They offered me the position permanently if I wanted it."

"Then you aren't—"

"Well, it isn't as though I was fired or anything, but I did lose access to certain powers in order to stay here full-time."

He kissed her palm. "You were willing to give up so much for me...for all of us?"

Her smile dazzled him with its brilliance. "I kept the most important thing. Love is too important to ever allow any to be wasted. We'll all share in that love and it will grow and grow. Maybe our love will help others to better understand."

He hugged her to him, while Travis still clung to her. Chris, Brenda and Sally joined them.

The Bishop children had a mother once again...and daddy had his angel.

*   *   *   *   *

Sometimes you find the most unexpected things
under the mistletoe—and on your doorstep!

Coming Home

International Bestselling Authors
Helen Bianchin
Lucy Gordon
Rebecca Winters

Join three favorite authors for this heartwarming new
anthology containing three delicious tales about coming
home for the holidays…with a few surprises!

Look for it November 2004!

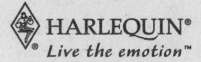

HARLEQUIN®
Live the emotion™

www.eHarlequin.com

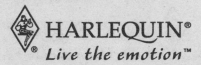

Return to Trueblood, Texas, with this brand-new novel of thrilling romantic suspense…

CHARLOTTE
DOUGLAS
Lover Under Cover

P.I. Dean Harding's search for the mother of an abandoned baby leads him to an Austin, Texas, hospital—and to Dr. Kate Purvis, a secretive OB who knows more than she's telling. So Dean goes undercover, hoping to get information in a more personal way.

Finders Keepers: bringing families together

Available in September 2004.

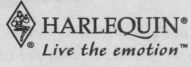